The Pen Pal

Holly Copella

To Mark Werner
Rock on!

ACKNOWLEDGMENTS

Copella Books: First Paperback Edition 2016
Printed by CreateSpace, An Amazon.com Company
Cover Artist: Daniela Owergoor
Dani-owergoor.deviantart.com

PUBLISHER'S NOTE

Chapter One

Several police cars were parked outside the abandoned, dilapidated building. The old warehouse was located on a quiet corner within the small town of Linville. The building had seen better days. Most of the windows were either boarded up or shattered and siding gave away to rusted metal beams. The broken doors to the entrance were roped off with bold, yellow police line meant to keep people out. Despite being a quiet area, nosy neighbors were already collecting at the sight of so many police cars in one area. Their flashing lights attracted them like a calling beacon. Locals knew it was something serious when nearly every Linville police cruiser was gathered in one location.

The second floor of the warehouse offered a magnificent view through broken glass windows to an overgrown lot littered with old tires and rusted machinery. The nearly empty second floor contained a few tattered sofas, battered chairs, and what was almost certainly a dead body beneath a white, blood-soaked sheet. Half a dozen police officers swarmed the area while the official photographer took several photos of the crime scene. Blood spatters painted the floor around the body, which had been placed within a symbol drawn in blood. A well-dressed man in suit stepped into the doorway and was immediately stopped by a young, lanky police officer.

"Sorry, Sir," Deputy Hunt announced with a slight crackle in his voice. "This is an official crime scene."

It was obvious the deputy was overwhelmed by what lay hidden beneath the blood-soaked sheet. The well-dressed newcomer flashed his badge and FBI credentials, showing disinterest toward the inexperienced officer.

"Agent Harris Slade, FBI," he casually announced without emotion and immediately replaced his badge to his jacket pocket almost as if performing a magic trick.

The young, ill-equipped police officer immediately fidgeted, reflecting his somewhat clueless nature, and stood aside, allowing Slade to enter. Agent Harris Slade was a moderately handsome, athletically built man in his mid-thirties with short dark hair and a clean-shaven face. Although not a big man, his arrogance made him seem larger than his less than average height. His imposing presence filled the room and commanded respect. Slade approached the body but appeared distracted, pausing only a few feet into the large room to peer at the nearby wall. He noted the strange, cryptic writing in blood.

Whatever the message, it was written in some unknown language. He stared at the wall and showed little reaction to the disturbing scene, although his hand subconsciously twitched. Slade finally turned away and approached the slightly out of shape, middle-aged police officer hovering over the blood-soaked sheet covering the unfortunate corpse. The sheriff's blank stare and knitted brows conveyed his inability to handle the situation presented before him. Slade paused before Sheriff Gruber, who broke out of his trance and finally looked at the man standing before him.

Sheriff Gruber was as much out of place at a murder crime scene as his girthy midsection was in his uniform. Although somewhat out of shape, the sheriff maintained a well-groomed appearance. He was clean-shaven and kept his slightly thinning, light brown hair cut short. Gruber eyed Slade and immediately puffed out his chest to display the importance of his status. His uniform buttons showed less strain as he held in his round belly. His thumbs comfortably slipped beneath his holster in a relaxed position, although he was anything but relaxed.

"This is a crime scene," Gruber announced in a gruff, yet rattled tone by what he had already witnessed beneath the bloodied sheet. "You can't be here."

Slade again performed his magic trick by flashing his badge and making it disappear into his inner jacket pocket. He showed little reaction to the sheriff's attitude.

"Agent Slade," he announced flatly. "FBI."

Gruber immediately fidgeted at the brief sight of the badge, reluctantly allowing his shoulders to sage with defeat to Slade's authority. His uniform buttons again strained beneath his relaxed midsection. He tugged on his gun holster in order to return it to its original more comfortable location beneath his round midsection.

"I'm Sheriff Gruber," he introduced himself while eying Slade. "You feds sure are fast. I'm certainly not complaining, you understand." Gruber resumed staring at the covered body, obviously still contemplating his next move. The small town sheriff was in desperate need of direction.

"There's a very sick man out there butchering women, Sheriff," Slade casually informed him even though that was already evident by the crime scene. "Every moment counts when it comes to catching guys like this." He gave a slight nod to the bloodied sheet. "May I?"

Gruber reluctantly nodded. "Yeah, of course."

The sheriff seemingly held his breath and pulled back the sheet to expose the mutilated young, naked woman. Her long, flowing red hair was now matted with blood against her carefully sliced skin. The once beautiful woman had the same strange writing carved into her chest, abdomen, and thighs. The odd carved words, now dried with blood, contained a certain refinement in their appearance. Due to lack of blood, it was evident most of the mutilation took place after the woman was already dead. Although the outcome remained the same, it was some comfort knowing the woman hadn't suffered through the torture of being carved as she had.

"Looks like he's writing a biography on human tablets," the sheriff muttered and appeared almost sickened by the sight. "No idea what it says." He attempted to look anywhere but at the body, having seen enough when he first arrived.

Slade knelt alongside the dead woman and studied her a long, silent moment. Apart from the carvings, there were no defensive wounds. Although she wasn't currently bound, her wrists and ankles were moderately bruised from whatever material her killer had used to keep her subdued. Forensics would undoubtedly reveal the material was duct tape. The amount of bruising indicated she'd had plenty of time to fight her binding. Cause of death was easily identified by her crudely torn throat, which contained a large amount of blood. The injury to her neck almost suggested she'd been attacked by some wild animal, but that wasn't the case.

"We haven't officially identified her yet, but some of the deputies think she was a waitress at the tavern," Gruber informed him. "Her clothing and any personal effects she may have had on her haven't been found. We're still searching the building."

Slade studied the dead woman carefully, taking in her injuries as well as her features. "Very beautiful--" he announced softly while trailing off. After he'd finished his visual inspection, he stood then cast a glance at the sheriff. "Don't you think?"

Gruber appeared somewhat uncomfortable by the question then reluctantly nodded in agreement. "Yeah," he muttered under his breath and cast a slight nod at the body. "She was quite a looker before he got to her."

"They all were," Slade casually informed him. "All his victims are young, attractive women in their early twenties with reddish hair." He eyed the sheriff while raising a brow. "None shorter than 5'4; none taller than 5'7."

The sheriff immediately shifted, revealing his discomfort. "It's him, isn't it?" he asked with a tone of dread. "It's the guy responsible for those killings over the past year in towns throughout the county. The one they call the Pen Pal."

"Oh, most definitely," Slade replied with little reaction then looked back at the dead woman. "He's killed nearly a dozen women in the surrounding area. Now he's picked your little town." He inhaled deeply then pulled the bloody sheet back over the body. "He has quite the artistic flare." He straightened and set his eyes back on the sheriff. "Always leaves them naked but never molests them." Slade cocked his head to the side and studied the sheriff. "Why do you suppose that is, Sheriff Gruber?"

"Impotence," Gruber suggested almost sounding confident while proudly throwing his shoulders back and standing tall. "Homosexual maybe?"

Slade shrugged in response. "Maybe it's just against the rules."

The sheriff gave him a puzzled look. "Against the rules?" he suddenly asked with surprise, again allowing his body to sage. "What rules?"

"Precisely what we need to find out," Slade replied with little emotion. "Does he kill for pleasure, out of necessity, or is it sacrificial in nature?"

"You think this is the work of a satanic cult?"

Slade turned and indicated the bloody writing on the wall, the symbol surrounding the body, and the wavy nubs of what had once been candles. "Has the atmosphere of a satanic ritual," he replied then gave the sheriff a stern, serious look. "He strikes in a series of three, choosing his victims very carefully, and then goes dormant for a few months."

"What number is this one?" the sheriff felt a curious need to ask.

"She's the first of three."

The sheriff stared at Slade with a look of horror on his face. "So you're saying there's a chance we'll have two more murders like this one?"

"I can almost guarantee he already has his next target picked out," Slade informed him. "Some poor, unsuspecting redheaded woman has already crossed paths with our killer. She just doesn't know it yet."

"So what do we do?" the sheriff nearly gasped, realizing he was in over his head.

"Follow procedure," Slade replied. "Call in the state police for assistance with the investigation. While autopsies are being performed and tests run, I'll be out there trying to track down his next victim."

"You're not heading up the investigation yourself?" the sheriff asked with surprise. "This is a heavy Irish area. Do you know how many redheaded women live in this town?"

"I need to stop this guy before he goes dormant again," Slade informed him. "I can't wait for protocol. The state police and homicide detective can assist you with the investigation. You build your case against him, but I need to go out there and find him while there's still time."

Sheriff Gruber slowly nodded. "I understand," he replied while shifting slightly and drew a nervous breath. "You do what you have to do. Go rogue for all I care, if that's what needs to be done. I just don't want to know about it."

"Don't worry, Sheriff," Slade announced and offered a tiny smile. "You won't."

Chapter Two

It was later that Thursday afternoon. The rustic Linville Town Theater had seen better days, but its vintage appearance for many was part of its charm. Tired worn seats from decades past, outdated carpeting along the aisles, and the bold red stage curtain screamed true theater experience. As the sound of slightly crackling music played over house speakers, several actors and actresses in their street clothing danced across the old, well-constructed stage. An attractive redheaded woman in her early twenties, Beth Reisler, was front center for a short solo dance routine. Beth was slender yet built athletic, as most dancers were. Her long, wavy red hair was pulled back into a young woman's ponytail, swinging and swishing with her body as she danced. The dance routine ended with a young man in his mid-twenties gracefully dipping Beth backward. Dawson Hayes held Beth daringly low as the music ended.

Dawson was every theater actress's dream come true. He was a handsome, sexy Latino man with flawless, bronzed complexion and silky dark hair begging to be rumpled. His athletic build combined the right amount of muscles to his toned body. His broad shoulders held up his large chest containing a light coating of chest hair. His sexy, sultry dance moves combined with his deep

Columbian accent was almost more than any woman could refuse. Despite his perfect presence, Beth's eyes locked on his showed no hint of attraction.

"And cut," a voice called out from the darkness of the auditorium.

Beth was quick to pull away from the handsome man and put some distance between them. The director, who had been lurking several rows back from center stage, approached from the dark auditorium as the actors and actresses on stage relaxed and watched the impressive man. The director, Tyler Henley, was nearly six feet tall with an athletic build from years spent on stage procuring his acting career prior to his directing debut. Although in his late thirties, he maintained a much younger appearance with his youthful choice in attire and a younger man's shoulder length sandy brown hair. His excessively calm demeanor made him the perfect director. There was never any yelling, and he had a way of bringing the actors around to his way of thinking without being excessively forceful. Tyler clapped loudly several times as he approached then paused before stage.

"That was just about perfect," Tyler informed them cheerfully. "We'll break for dinner and continue with the second half when we get back."

Everyone appeared relieved, having pleased their directing overlord, and began to disperse from the stage for a well-deserved break. Beth started to head backstage when Dawson hurried after her, caught her arm, and stopped her. She appeared annoyed by his hand clutching her arm and glared her disapproval. He immediately released her arm, knowing the look he'd received, and attempted a sympathetic smile.

"Come on, Beth. It's been a week," Dawson playfully pouted in his sexy Columbian accent and offered his best charming smile, revealing excessively white teeth. "You know it kills me when we're apart. When are you going to forgive me?"

Her glare should have conveyed her thoughts, but Dawson didn't seem to take hints well. "Forgiving you is not a problem, Dawson," she casually informed him while giving him an irritated once over, "but that doesn't mean I intend to go out with you ever again."

"That's not fair," he protested in a boyish hissy fit.

"Neither was you going home with that little tramp from the bar," Beth snapped hotly while folding her arms across her chest then arched her commanding brows for added effect. "Maybe you'll learn your lesson for your next girlfriend."

One of the other young actresses approached from backstage, obviously having heard the interaction, and glared at Dawson with the same impatient look.

"Give it up, Dawson," Loni Fritz growled with annoyance as she too folded her arms across her chest and maintained the same firm stance as Beth had. "You screwed up. It's over, and she doesn't want to see you anymore."

Dawson glared at the young, attractive woman resembling an attack dog standing alongside Beth. Loni was a beauty in her own rights, but she wasn't the stunning woman Beth was. Loni was slightly shorter and, although not overweight by any means, she was more muscular, giving her a slightly stocky appearance. For rehearsal, she too wore her dirty blond hair in a ponytail but not nearly as high on her head as Beth's. It gave her a slightly more mature look even though the two women were actually the same age.

Dawson wasn't happy with Loni's interruption and didn't mind expressing his feelings. "This doesn't concern you, Loni," he snarled back, losing the sexiness in his tone.

"Beth's my friend," she snapped while maintaining her Pit Bull glare. "You better believe it concerns me."

"Beth--" Dawson attempted to protest then looked at her for support.

Beth's look remained unsympathetic. Dawson frowned then stormed backstage and into the wings. Loni watched him leave then turned toward Beth while shaking her head.

"What a jerk," Loni scoffed.

"He's just misguided," Beth reluctantly replied with a sigh while allowing her arms to fall to her sides. "He's used to getting his way, but I'm not like his past girlfriends. He won't walk all over me."

"That's a good attitude," Loni cheerfully announced and relaxed her stance as well. "I'm proud of you for sticking to your guns. I know that can't be easy, especially when a man looks as good as Dawson does."

"I'm just glad he hadn't heard about my date with Jerome tonight," she remarked with a soft groan. "That really would've sent him over the edge."

"You've been so secretive about your upcoming date." Loni grinned deviously while admiring her friend. "So, who is the mystery man?"

"I'm not entirely sure. He's a mystery to me too," Beth informed her friend while hiding her childlike smile. "We met on-line in a singles chat room, so I haven't really gotten to know him all that well. We've only exchanged a few pictures. Jerome was reluctant to do video chat for our first meeting, so I asked him to pick me up here after rehearsal tonight. He planned on showing up near the end and catching some of rehearsal." She studied her friend while attempting to hide the color in her cheeks. "Maybe you'd like to stick around afterwards and meet him."

Loni playfully pouted. "I'd love too, but I'm meeting Leonard at Jerry's Tavern after rehearsal," she replied with a dreary sigh then turned enthusiastic. "Maybe we can meet you later. Where are you going? Please tell me someplace other than Jerry's Tavern." She groaned and shook her head. "You'd swear it's the only bar in the entire town."

"That's because it practically is," Beth remarked with little enthusiasm. "The better places are too expensive or clear on the other side of town. Honestly, I don't want to chance running into Dawson at the tavern, so I hope he suggests someplace else." She sank into her own world a moment then finally met her friend's gaze. "I can text you later when I find out."

"That'd be great. Leonard's a bit of a stick-in-the-mud when it comes to going anywhere not walking distance from the apartment, but I'm sure I can get him to leave Jerry's and go someplace else if I tell him we're meeting you and your friend." She considered the comment then fidgeted. "Well, he'll agree to it as long as I offer to pay for the cab." Loni eyed her friend and then grinned lustfully. "So?" she announced. "Is he cute? You said you exchanged pictures."

"Judging by the pictures he'd sent me, he's very cute," Beth replied gleefully. "He's intelligent too. Almost poetic." She drifted into her own fantasy world. "He's mysterious and sinisterly charming."

"Hmm. Love him already," Loni cooed while raising her brows lustfully. "Let's just hope he's who he says he is. I have my reservations about on-line dating. I'm glad I never had to do it." She offered a sly smirk. "I mean, what can go wrong with on-line dating, right?" she teased.

"I know," Beth said with a reluctant sigh, "but it wasn't my intent. It just sort of happened."

"What does he do for a living?" Loni asked. "Did you at least ask?"

"Well, he says he's a business executive," Beth replied, although she didn't seem convinced and fidgeted slightly. "I'm not sure what that exactly means. I'm sure I'll find out all the details tonight."

Loni giggled with a schoolgirl's delight. "Can't wait to meet him." She gently nudged her friend. "Come on, let's get something to eat."

"Where did you want to go?" Beth asked.

Loni groaned and rolled her eyes. "We're pressed for time and short on cash," she remarked with little enthusiasm and raised her brows in response. "Where do you think?"

Beth laughed softly. "I'm guessing Jerry's Tavern with the rest of the theater company."

"Bingo," Loni remarked then laughed.

As both women turned, they saw the tall, lanky janitor leaning on his broom just to the side of the curtain. He appeared to be watching them then immediately returned to his work when they directed their attention at him. He pushed his broom along the floor and headed backstage. Loni insecurely grabbed Beth's arm.

"There he is, leering again," she muttered. "God, he gives me the creeps."

"I'm sure he's harmless," Beth replied softly as they exited backstage as well.

"Yeah, sure," Loni remarked while releasing her arm. "Explain why he's always here, and why it always seems like he's watching me."

Beth offered a slight shrug. "Well, he does live above the theater, so that's probably why he's always here."

"Well, I, uh, fine," she scoffed with defeat. "But explain why he's always watching me."

"You sort of do leave a trail of empty coffee cups and snack wrappers behind you," Beth replied timidly.

Loni glared at her friend, not humored by the comment. Beth laughed softly and hugged her. As they headed toward the side doors that would take them into the parking lot, both women stopped when they heard soft male voices. They exchanged looks in silent question then took a few steps down the hallway. The voices silenced, although they had been coming from the back storage room. Loni uncertainly followed Beth closer to the doorway. Beth entered the doorway and nearly collided with a tall, thin man wearing tattered clothing. Both women screamed and jumped back with alarm. The homeless man bolted past them and ran for the back exit. The dirty, scruffy man in his late forties was enough to frighten both women. Loni grabbed her cell phone and started dialing the police. The janitor suddenly appeared from the back room, saw them, and stared at them with surprise.

"What's going on?" he suddenly demanded.

"There was an intruder," Beth cried out.

"Who? Derek?" the janitor scoffed. "He's no intruder. I invited him to share my lunch. I didn't think nobody would mind. He's harmless." He shook his head with annoyance. "You probably scared him half to death."

"I know the feeling," Loni remarked and returned her phone to her purse. "Should you really be inviting him in here?"

"Tyler said it was okay as long as everyone was out to lunch," the janitor insisted with a slightly offended look. "I'm telling you; he's harmless."

Beth nudged Loni. "Come on, let's go."

Chapter Three

Jerry's Tavern seemed to be the only game in town when it came to lunch. There weren't many options close to the theater, and nearly the entire theater company ended up going there for lunch and sometimes even drinks together in the evening after rehearsal. The tavern was particularly crowded for lunchtime, leaving Beth and Loni little choice but to sit at the bar. It was either the bar or join Dawson at his table. Both women opted for the bar instead. As they made themselves comfortable on the tall stools, the owner, Jerry, approached them from behind the bar. He usually worked the bar during the afternoon, when the place was less busy. Although, that wasn't the case this particular afternoon.

"Hello my lovelies," Jerry cheerfully greeted the women. "The usual?"

"Uh, not for me," Loni replied while grinning slyly. "I'm feeling adventurous. Make my dressing French instead of ranch today."

Jerry laughed and was about to walk away, having their order to memory, when Beth spoke up.

"Rather busy this afternoon, aren't you?" Beth asked, forcing Jerry to stop and turn to face her.

"I don't want to ruin your lunch," he announced then casually leaned on the bar facing them, "but you'll hear soon enough from my gossiping waitress."

"You shouldn't talk about your sister that way," Loni teased with a grin.

"What is it?" Beth asked while looking around, sensing the strange mood of those in the tavern.

"They found a woman murdered in that old, abandoned warehouse on the next block," Jerry informed them while straightening. He indicated the crowd. "Half the patrons here are with news stations or newspapers, and the other half are local busybodies."

"A woman was murdered?" Beth gasped while staring at the bartender with horror. "Oh, my God. What happened? Do they know who was killed? Do they know who did it?"

"They're not saying much," Jerry replied while subconsciously wiping the bar with his dirty towel. "I just hope it wasn't Wendy. She went missing a few days ago."

"Wendy?" Loni suddenly gasped. "Wendy your waitress Wendy?"

He nodded. "Everyone assumed she ran off with her boyfriend, but now we're not so sure." He sighed softly. "At least, I hope that's where she went."

Jerry received several waves from others at the bar and hurried away to tend to his customers. Loni and Beth exchanged looks of disbelief.

"Wendy?" Loni gasped softly and stared at nothing in particular. "I don't believe it."

"I wonder when it happened," Beth remarked, sharing the same disbelief. "What if it happened when she was leaving work? The theater is only a couple blocks from here. You know how dark that parking lot can be at night."

"No one knows if it was actually Wendy they found," Loni replied. "Besides, you have nothing to worry about. We usually leave together."

"Well, even so," Beth announced and sighed deeply. "I think it's time to start carrying that Taser my father gave me. Won't do me any good sitting in the drawer at home."

Loni didn't seem to be paying attention to her friend and suddenly slipped back into reality. "Did Wendy even have a boyfriend?" she suddenly asked. "I mean, we talked and stuff, but I don't remember her saying anything about dating anyone in particular."

"There was that one guy who came in here all the time," Beth replied. "What was his name?"

Loni gave her a sly look. "Every guy here comes here all the time," she remarked.

"You know the guy," Beth groaned softly. "Wavy hair, yay tall, funny sort of guy. You know who I mean. Nerdy in a cute sort of way."

Loni snapped her fingers and pointed at Beth while grinning. "Yeah, what's his name!"

"Yeah, him."

Loni then sank into thought and studied her friend while tilting her head. "Was Wendy the waitress Dawson did in the back coat closet?"

Beth refrained from rolling her eyes and snorted a soft laugh. "No, that was Heidi, Jerry's sister." She then considered the comment and frowned. "But I wouldn't doubt Dawson did Wendy too. With the way she flirted with him--"

"Wendy did flirt with a lot of men, didn't she?" Loni then remarked and eyed her friend. "You don't suppose one of the guys from the bar--?"

"I'd put my money on some jealous girlfriend first," Beth replied without waiting for her to finish the question.

"Yeah," Loni nearly gasped as her eyes widened. "Remember that freaky chick who came in here that one time? Sat in the back corner with her friend. A guy made a pass at her, and she nearly took his head off."

"Yeah, I think I saw her with what's his name," Beth announced. "You know; the nerdy one."

Loni was about to respond when she hesitated and looked past Beth to a man seated near them at the bar. He sipped his beer while casually keeping an eye on them. He didn't even attempt to hide the fact that he'd been listening to their conversation, indicated by the smirk on his face.

"Do you mind?" Loni nearly demanded, slipping back into protective Pit Bull mode.

The man shrugged while maintaining his humor. "Not at all," he announced. "It's not often I get to hear gossip from women I don't know about women they think they know yet no one seems to know who the hell they're gossiping about."

Beth stared at the strange man with surprise as her mouth hung open. The slightly balding man in his mid-thirties was intimidating looking with a solid build and a two-inch scar along the outer side of his right eye that traveled down his cheek. His worn leather jacket had seen better days and possibly some combat. Loni was about to come back at him with a smart remark when Beth kicked her under the bar. She yelped slightly and glared at her friend. Beth glared back with a look that clearly scolded her, forbidding her from getting into any sort of debate with the tough looking man. Loni frowned and looked away, abiding by her friend's silent wish. The intimidating man laughed softly and continued to drink his beer.

Chapter Four

Backstage later that night, the theater company had finished rehearsal and nearly everyone had gone home for the evening. Beth paced the small cleared area between the racks of costumes and stage props. She glanced at her watch several times then paused by one of the make-up tables, glanced in the mirror, and gave her red hair a flirty toss. Through the mirror, she saw the janitor standing several feet away watching her through dark, beady eyes. Beth let out a startled scream and spun around, nearly knocking the make-up kit from the table. When she looked back, the janitor was already pushing his broom away from the backstage area. She held her head a moment and exhaled softly.

"I concede, Loni," she muttered softly more to herself. "He's creepy."

She looked at her watch and frowned. It was nearly half an hour past the time she was supposed to meet her date, and the front doors would now be locked, so he wasn't getting in even if he did show up. Beth sighed with defeat and left through the side hall door into the corridor. She walked along the corridor and entered the old, glass front lobby. She scanned the area beyond the glass to see if

Jerome was waiting for her outside. When she didn't find him waiting on the sidewalk beyond the glass walls, Beth again glanced at her watch and paced the length of the large lobby. The theater was now eerily silent and it was apparent nearly everyone had gone. She turned and nearly collided with Tyler. Beth jumped with surprise, letting out a startled, shrill cry, and then smiled with a slight laugh while holding her chest.

"Tyler, you startled me."

Tyler had been unaffected by their near collision, maintaining his calm demeanor. He hid his grin, apparently amused that he'd startled the young woman without half trying.

"This place has that certain spooky appeal at night once everyone's gone home," he teased. Tyler then looked at his watch and eyed her suspiciously. "Why are you still here? I thought everyone had gone home."

"My date is late," she announced and subconsciously frowned at the comment.

"Oh," he replied not seeming worried. "Did you need a ride somewhere?"

"No," she remarked with a dreary sigh. "I'm sure he'll be here soon."

Somehow, Tyler didn't appear convinced but easily let it go. "Okay," he responded with little emotion. "But if you need me for any reason, I'll be backstage a little while longer."

Beth smiled her appreciation and nodded. It was obvious he had been on his way out, being he had a reserved parking spot out front, but he wasn't about to leave her alone in the theater, particularly in the evening in a dead part of town. It just wasn't the sort of man he was, but keeping his concerns to himself *was* the sort of man he was. Tyler walked toward the back hall while Beth continued her pacing, feeling better knowing Tyler was around to keep an eye on her. A few minutes had passed when a clunk was heard from the auditorium, alerting Beth. She looked toward the closed auditorium doors and saw one door swaying slightly. She appeared puzzled and stared a moment longer. She knew it wasn't Tyler. He'd gone into the back hallway and couldn't have made it around that fast. Something then occurred to her, and she felt some hostility while glaring toward the auditorium doors.

"Dawson, is that you?"

There was no response. Beth approached the doors, slowly pulled them open, and uncertainly stood in the doorway to the dimly lit auditorium. She held the door open as she felt around the wall for the light switch. A shadowy figure appeared behind her in the dim lighting from the lobby. As if sensing something, Beth tensed and started to turn. She was suddenly grabbed from behind and a cloth was placed over her nose and mouth. Beth fought the hand and the cloth, jabbing the person from behind in the midsection with her elbow. She broke free from her attacker and stumbled down the aisle while gasping for her breath. She clutched her head and felt dizzy from the chemicals on the cloth, which had to be chloroform. She stumbled toward the lit stage and possible help.

"Tyler!"

Her legs weakened and started to give beneath her as she nearly collapsed before the stage. Beth looked behind her, half expecting to see her attacker standing over her, but he wasn't there. She heard movement from the dark auditorium as Tyler hurried onto the stage from backstage. He wore a look of concern having heard her frightened cries.

"Beth?"

"Tyler," she gasped. "Thank God!"

Without hesitation, Tyler leaped off the stage only a few feet from her. Beth gathered her strength and attempted to reach him. A shadowy figure jumped out of the darkness and tackled Tyler to the floor. Despite his surprise attack, Tyler fought the man on top of him with stunning reflexes.

"Run, Beth!"

As Tyler fought the man on top of him in the darkness of the aisle, his attacker raised a knife from his position over him. Beth saw the knife clutched in the man's gloved hand. She gasped with horror and, with all her strength, ran to help Tyler.

"Tyler, no!"

Before she could reach him, she witnessed the killer plunging the knife repeatedly into Tyler as he cried out in agony while still fighting his attacker. As blood flew off the dagger with each thrust, Beth knew Tyler's fate had already been sealed. She screamed as she turned and ran back toward the main lobby doors. Her strength was slowly returning possibly due to the adrenaline now coursing through her body. The killer straightened near the stage with his knife dripping blood, hesitated only a moment, and then chased after her. He swiftly gained on her. She was almost to the doors when he suddenly tackled her to the floor. Beth screamed, managing to kick him off her, and sprang to her feet.

As she reached for the door, her attacker thrust the knife for her leg and missed, striking the doorframe instead. Beth screamed and leaped away from the door, now blocked by the crouching killer. She scanned the dimly lit auditorium to the back exit sign and bolted down the dark side aisle. As she looked back while running, she saw her attacker was gone. All she saw was light from the main entrance as the door slowly closed. Had he given up his pursuit and took off before more help arrived? Beth stopped just before the side door exit near the stage, revealing her distrust and apprehension. She looked around the dark auditorium a moment longer.

Her eyes then fell upon the door before her. Could he have made it across the lobby and down the back hallway in those few seconds? She nervously backed away from the door then turned and ran onto the stage. The side exit door was suddenly thrown open, indicating she'd been correct and had avoided an ambush. She screamed and darted backstage. Beth ran past the wardrobe area and toward the back fire door, which would bring her into the alley leading to the back parking lot. She skidded into the door, unable to stop, then quickly recovered and attempted to pull it open. It wouldn't open!

She heard a clunk from backstage, indicating he was close. Beth turned around and looked across the dimly lit backstage area. She didn't see anything, but in the darkness, he could have been anywhere waiting to strike. Beth remained close to the wall and watched the area surrounding her while inching her way toward the second door on the far side. She moved closer to the second door near the wardrobe racks and old props. Then she saw it! The emergency fire pull alarm was only three feet away from her alongside the door.

She leaped for the fire alarm and swiftly pulled it. Relief flooded through her body as the fire alarm wailed loudly, indicating help would soon be on its way. As she turned, she saw the dark blur of her attacker leaping from the wardrobe rack. He cast her roughly against the side door. Beth screamed and fought against the powerful man attempting to restrain her. Between the dim lighting and fierceness of her struggle, she was unable to see his face. He punched her in the head with enough force to daze her. She became excessively dizzy and slowly slid down the emergency exit door. The last thing she saw was the hazy image of her attacker hovering over her.

✝

The fire alarm continued to wail for several minutes from within the old theater. It was loud enough to alert anyone outside for several blocks as well. Dawson hurried for the side alley entrance, having approached from the back parking lot while fumbling with his keys. The alarm had alerted him to whatever had happened inside. The side door was thrown open, almost striking him, and the homeless man, Derek, nearly collided with him. Dawson jumped back with surprise and stared at the homeless man, who could only stare back with a look of horror on his dirt-covered face. He had blood on his otherwise clean hands.

"Hey!" Dawson cried out, his gruff Columbian accent adding to the threatening tone.

Derek bolted past him and ran through the alley toward the back parking lot. Dawson eyed the slowly closing door that would automatically lock once it had shut. He caught the door and hurried inside. Dawson only took a moment to look around before making his way through the backstage area. A faint gasp caught his attention. He hurried onto stage and saw an unfamiliar man crouching over Tyler's blood-soaked, mutilated body. Dawson couldn't look away from the frightening condition of their director then finally looked at the man standing over him. The man straightened and stared at Dawson while trembling.

"He's still alive," the man gasped with fear in his voice. "We need an ambulance."

Dawson leaped off stage and hurried toward them while eyeing the man suspiciously. He then removed his cell phone and pressed 911. Tyler's breathing was shallow. The fact that he was still alive after the brutal assault was nothing short of a miracle.

"Who are you?" Dawson demanded with distrust, not about to let the man out of his sight.

"I'm Jerome," the stranger replied nervously. "I came to pick up Beth, but I was running late. My cell phone wasn't working. The lobby door was unlocked, so I let myself in."

Jerome was a tall, well-built man in his late twenties with flowing golden-brown hair nearly touching his shoulders. Nowhere near as handsome as Dawson, he was attractive in his own rights and built far more muscular. Jerome obviously saw the way Dawson was staring at him while awaiting the call to be answered. Jerome shook his head defensively.

"Hey, I swear, I found him like this," Jerome announced quickly. "There was another guy. He looked like a homeless man. He ran when I saw him."

Tyler's shallow breathing ended with a soft gasp, catching the attention of both men. The back door busted open to reveal several firemen and the officer on duty, Deputy Hunt. Dawson and Jerome both turned to face the first responders hurrying down the aisle. Their conclusion to what they thought happened was evident on their faces and by the way they stared at the two, seemingly guilty looking men. Deputy Hunt stopped in the aisle with a look of horror on his face as he stared at the mutilated man. He nervously ran his fingers through his hair and started to tremble. The firemen wasted little time running for the mortally wounded man bleeding out on the tacky, old carpet. Both men stepped aside and allowed the firemen room to work, but it was obvious Tyler was gone. Jerome and Dawson then looked at one another as if coming to the same conclusion.

"Where's Beth?" Dawson suddenly asked.

Both men looked around, panic sweeping over them. They ran for the stage yelling her name. Deputy Hunt remained frozen in the aisle while staring at the dead man on the floor halfway across the auditorium as the alarm continued to blare.

Chapter Five

Thursday night was lady's night at Jerry's Tavern. It was already midnight and the bar was swarming with men anticipating a strong turnout of women. Despite drink specials, the ratio was still four-to-one not in the men's favor. One table in particular was home to two sedate looking men. Dawson and Jerome were already drunk beyond comprehension. The waitress avoided their table, since they had been cut off due to their current condition. Neither man spoke much after their ordeal with the dead director, Beth's disappearance, and excessive questioning by the homicide detective.

Two attractive women in their early twenties sat at a table toward the back. They shared a Kamikaze pitcher, which was nearly empty, explaining the laughter coming from the two women. One look at the attractive Gillian Foxwood and it was easy to imagine her string of jilted lovers. The gorgeous redhead had an impressive body to match her cover model face. Her cleavage and perfectly rounded buttocks were admired by both men and women. She was dressed to kill and the list of men happy to oblige was lengthy. Her friend wasn't nearly as impressive, dressed in her favorite jeans and casual shirt, which revealed absolutely nothing. Jolynn Raynard had silky, long reddish brown hair that she chose to wear in a casual ponytail, portraying the typical girl next door. Young, sweet, and innocent looking. She'd freely admit to one out of three. Jolynn glanced at her watch and noted it was just after midnight. She picked up her nearly empty glass and eyed her giddy friend.

"Time to go, Gillian," Jolynn stated, leaving no room for argument.

Gillian groaned with disgust. "I'm not ready to leave yet," she pouted. "Another hour."

"We both have work tomorrow," Jolynn reminded. "Unlike you, I'd like to be able to function. You don't know what I have to deal with."

"Mr. McQueen isn't that bad," Gillian announced with a groan. "Give the poor guy a break. I hear his wife is cheating on him."

"She's not cheating on him," Jolynn insisted then shook her head. "I don't understand how you get so much gossip on the people I work with."

"Dan stopped by last Saturday night," Gillian replied in a slightly drunk tone. "He told me all about Mr. McQueen's wife stepping out on him."

"Shows what either of you know," Jolynn informed her. "His wife works out-of-town three days a week. That's why she's not around much." She considered the comment then sulked silently. "Lucky her. She gets a four-day weekend every week. I'd kill for that schedule."

Gillian considered the comment and nodded. "You know, I think I would too." She eyed her friend despite her inability to focus on her. "Why would Dan spread those rumors?"

"Why? Because he's Dan," Jolynn boldly announced. "You've met the guy. He'll do or say anything to impress women. Ironically, they either love him or hate him."

"I think he's a little creep," Gillian remarked bluntly. "But he's not all that bad, I suppose."

"I haven't made up my mind yet," Jolynn replied. "I keep thinking he'll drop the act and morph into a normal person."

"Did you know he asked me out like three times?"

Jolynn rolled her eyes. "What else is new," she muttered. "He asks me out every other day."

The waitress, Heidi, approached their table with a full pitcher of Kamikazes and set it down between them. Jolynn looked at the young waitress with surprise.

"Oh, no," she quickly announced. "We didn't order this. We need to head home."

"Drinks on the gentlemen," Heidi announced with a lustful smile.

Gillian looked across the bar at the two men slouched over their drinks. Her eyes sparkled as a smile crossed her face.

"Isn't that Dawson Hayes, the theater actor?" Gillian announced with renewed enthusiasm.

The waitress glanced across the room toward the bar and noted the sloppy drunk men on the verge of passing out.

"Uh, yes, it is," the waitress replied. "But they didn't buy the drinks." She indicated the table near the back of the bar. "This is from those two men."

Gillian and Jolynn glanced across the bar in the direction the waitress indicated. Two men sat in the corner table. One was excessively large and muscular, while the other was shorter and moderately geeky in appearance. Baxter was built like a professional football player. His dirty blonde hair was nearly shoulder length, his thin lips twisted into a devious, twisted smile, and his beady eyes tore through them like a tasty, sweet snack. Carl, the shorter of the two, was a moderately geeky looking guy in his late twenties with dark, curly hair and glasses. He was non-impressive and possibly twice as boring. Gillian smiled at the men and waved drunkenly while talking to Jolynn through the side of her mouth.

"I can already tell you which one you're stuck with," Gillian teased.

Jolynn caught Gillian's wrist by her shirt cuff and pulled it down. "That's not happening, Gillian," she firmly announced. "We both have to work tomorrow. It's time to go. Give him your phone number if you absolutely must, but then we're leaving."

Gillian glared at Jolynn and sneered her disapproval. "You're no fun."

Jolynn folded her arms across her chest and leaned back in her chair. "Maybe not, but my ex-boyfriend didn't just walk through the door either."

Her friend whirled around in her chair to see the last man she'd hoped to see that night. Larry immediately honed in on their table, smiled brilliantly, and approached. Gillian's ex-boyfriend was about as handsome as one would imagine for the beautiful woman. He had golden-brown hair that was just long enough to flow, a broad muscular chest, and straight white teeth bright enough to blind any woman. Unfortunately, he had an ego to match his perfect existence, and he was her co-worker just to make things twice as messy when she broke up with him. Gillian rolled her eyes and groaned, now that her perfect night was ruined.

"Ah, hell," she scoffed. "Let's go."

Gillian and Jolynn stood just in time to see Larry approaching their table from the front and the two strangers approaching from the back. Jolynn groaned softly and covered her eyes while shaking her head.

"There's no way this is going to end well," she muttered softly more to herself.

†

Jolynn stirred restlessly beneath the covers on her bed within her mostly dark bedroom. She rolled onto her back with a groan and stared at the ceiling. The sound of a loudly creaking bed through the dividing wall was barely heard beyond Gillian's screams of ecstasy. Jolynn pulled her pillow over her head and screamed into it.

Chapter Six

Friday morning. The living room within Jolynn's small, tidy apartment was barely big enough to fit a loveseat and chair. The two-bedroom apartment was efficient, functional, and cheap for two young women struggling to make it on their own. Jolynn left the bathroom while hastily putting her long hair up into a sloppy ponytail. Jolynn was comfortable in her familiar surroundings and that's where she firmly drew the line. The less she interacted with other people, the happier she was. She paused outside Gillian's closed bedroom door and considered whether to knock or not. It wouldn't be the first awkward moment being greeted by one of Gillian's overnight guests. Making sure her friend wasn't late for work again took priority over anyone's comfort. She drew a deep breath and vigorously knocked on the bedroom door, awaiting whatever surprise she'd find. Even if it meant being greeted by the occasional naked man.

"Come on, Gillian," Jolynn announced through the door. "You're going to be late *again*."

It was a standing joke, although Jolynn never found it that funny. Her best friend and roommate was forever late for work. More often than not, it was due to some poor decision she'd made the evening before, which was obviously the case last night. Whether staying out too late or carrying on with some co-worker, there was always some reason for Gillian to avoid getting to work on time. Jolynn continued past the bedroom door, hoping to avoid that awkward moment with Gillian's overnight company, and grabbed the television remote on her way to the open kitchen. She turned on the television as she approached the island counter. The news anchor covered the story about the murdered woman found in an abandoned building on the other side of town.

The bedroom door finally opened and a weary Gillian shuffled from her bedroom wearing her pink satin bathrobe covering her skimpy, sexy nightgown. She lazily picked up the remote control from the island counter and changed the channel to cartoons as she cast herself onto the plush loveseat. Jolynn turned and saw her disheveled friend looking worn, depressed, and more than likely hungover.

"You aren't even dressed," she firmly scolded her friend.

Although Jolynn was moderately surprised to see her friend still in her nightgown, she shouldn't have been. Gillian had a long, rough night, and Jolynn would know, because she suffered through having to listen to most of it.

"You're going to get into trouble if you're late again," Jolynn warned her.

"I'm calling in sick," Gillian pouted while sinking onto her back, draping her legs over the arm of the loveseat. "I can't possibly face work."

"Work or Larry?" Jolynn scoffed. "I can't believe you invited him back to the apartment. I warned you not to talk to him."

"You also warned me about dating co-workers," Gillian mocked without looking away from her cartoons. "Let's not start with the 'I told you so' business."

Jolynn casually leaned on the back of the loveseat and stared at her friend while raising an arrogant brow. "Well, I did," she remarked then groaned softly. "I suppose he snuck out early."

"It's what he does," she muttered with disgust. "He was out of my life, and I screwed up by inviting him back. Now I have to break up with him all over again." Gillian frowned and avoided looking at Jolynn. "He's going to tell everyone at work that we had sex last night. In graphic detail, I'm sure."

"You're going to need to go back to work eventually, so you'd better just deal with Larry now, face the embarrassment, and get it over with," Jolynn informed her.

"I will," she replied casually then sneered at the thought. "When it's legal to put a bullet in his head."

"Oh, stop with that," Jolynn scolded her friend as if she were a child. "Get dressed. You need to go to work. Get the awkward unpleasantness over with."

"No, I'm going to stay home, eat ice cream, and watch cartoons."

Jolynn shook her head and straightened with a defeated sigh. "I'd argue with you, but I'd be wasting my breath, and then I'd be late for work," she remarked. "I'll see you tonight."

Gillian waved without bothering to look back at her. Jolynn groaned softly, shook her head, and headed for the door.

Chapter Seven

Linville Hospital was relatively modern for the small town. The newly constructed building was smaller than most city hospitals, but it contained the necessary departments for the town's health care needs, which included radiology, surgery, and its own morgue. Within the basement, one of several frosted doors toward the end of the hall read *Medical Records*. The medical records room consisted of several aisles of large filing shelves and some stored items from the old hospital. Jolynn sat behind a stack of folders on her small, cluttered desk not far from the main door. She sorted through the folders and attempted to organize them. Jolynn worked alone in the peaceful basement room. The room was nearly soundproof, being mostly concrete block walls and cement floor. She worked in virtual silence, which was her preference. A young man in his early twenties with dark wavy hair entered with a rolling plastic cart piled high with stacks of folders. Dan rode the cart toward her desk with childlike glee.

"Incoming!"

Jolynn barely looked up, remaining unaffected by his attempt at juvenile humor. "It never ends," she remarked.

She wasn't really sure if she disliked Dan or just felt sorry for him. He was relatively handsome in an immature sort of way. He looked more like a computer whiz, conveying he was smarter than he actually was. Perhaps that explained the charm he held over other women. Some of the younger nurses were taken with his moderately intellectual look and fun-loving nature, but Jolynn felt he had no direction in life. He'd worked a dozen or more jobs in his short work career, and he'd already gotten into trouble at the hospital in the few months he'd been working there as well. Dan placed the files on the sole vacant spot on the corner of her desk and raised a clever brow while studying her.

"Your job must really suck," he chirped with enthusiasm. "No one ever sees you, and you're always up to your elbows in paperwork." He playfully jumped onto his cart and sat on it, swinging his legs like a hyperactive child while grinning at her.

"Actually, I enjoy paperwork, and I like the solitude," she casually informed him. "I'm a hermit."

Dan watched her work with more than a passing interest. Being a young man, he had a tendency to flirt with her as well as most of the single nurses and nursing assistants. She felt his eyes on her but attempted to avoid further conversation, since she knew where it usually led.

"I was wondering," he announced while shifting on the cart then grinned boyishly, "I have two tickets for the new show at the town theater. Maybe you'd like to go with me."

Jolynn glanced at him then returned to her piles of paperwork. It wasn't the first time he'd asked her out. He was notorious for asking out almost every single woman under thirty at the hospital.

"That's very nice of you, Dan," she replied politely, "but I can't."

Dan appeared offended by the rejection and jumped off his cart. "You know, I've asked you out six times, and six times you've said no," he boldly announced. "Are you ever going to go out with me?"

She looked up with surprise to his mild tantrum. She would have thought he'd be used to rejection, with as often as he asked her and other co-workers out.

"You're a nice guy, you really are, but I told you before, I don't date co-workers," she flatly reminded him then muttered more to herself, "My roommate recently reminded me why that's a good practice."

"That's cool. I understand," he announced casually although it was obvious he was insulted by the twisted way he smiled. "At least I don't have to waste my time asking anymore."

Dan turned with a little added vigor and left with his cart. His sudden hostility was slightly surprising. It was obvious something happened recently in the young man's life that made him less tolerant to rejection today. Jolynn shook her head with a sigh, grateful the drama had ended, and returned to her work. It wasn't worth getting involved in his emotional tirade, although she felt sorry for the next young woman to reject him.

Jolynn picked up a stack of folders, placed them on her own cart, and pushed it down a long row of file shelves. As she filed the folders, she heard someone enter the records room. Jolynn paused a moment and looked down the aisle with a curious tilt of her head. There was no usual greeting when someone was looking for her and the staff rarely roamed the file room without checking in with her first. She pushed her cart along the aisle to the end and collided with Harris Slade as he mysteriously appeared around the corner. The files toppled from her cart. Jolynn let out a startled scream to the sight of the unfamiliar although remarkably well-dressed man.

Slade appeared less startled and managed a tiny smirk. "I'm sorry," he announced with little sincerity.

Jolynn collected herself and attempted a polite response, despite already getting a feel for the stranger's less than charming personality.

"May I help you?"

Slade flashed his badge with amazing speed. "I'm Agent Slade with the FBI."

Jolynn watched the badge quickly fold back up and return to his inner jacket pocket in one fluid motion. Her eyes met his for a brief moment. Despite her suspicious nature, she couldn't help but notice he had the most stunning blue eyes. Blue eyes aside, Jolynn remained untrusting of the unfamiliar man claiming to be a federal agent.

"What can I do for you, Agent Slade?"

"I'm investigating a murder, and I need to look through some of your files," Slade casually informed her with an air of arrogance about him.

Her eyes didn't leave his as she remained unemotional and cool toward him. He seemed to take her stare as a challenge and refused to look away first.

"I don't mean to sound rude, Agent Slade," she announced firmly, "but I'll need approval from my supervisor before allowing you access to confidential files."

"I understand," he casually replied. "By all means, talk to your superior."

"If you could come back in ten minutes--"

"I'll wait," he curtly replied.

Slade turned and disappeared around the corner. Jolynn watched him vanish from the aisle and stared with astonishment. It had been a long time since she'd run into such a high level of arrogance. She remained untrusting as she stared after the strange man then gathered her fallen, scattered files and threw them on the cart with mild disgust.

Chapter Eight

Jolynn hurried back to her desk, now slightly flustered. To her surprise, Slade wasn't there. Jolynn looked around, becoming quickly annoyed. She snatched her phone from the desk and pressed a single button while looking around for any sign of the man. She then heard movement somewhere within the file room. He was snooping around without permission! Her irritation increased. Someone finally picked up on the other end.

"Mr. McQueen," she announced firmly into the phone. "Could you come down to the file room right away? I have a situation."

She awaited a response from her boss then hung up the phone and moved behind her desk. Jolynn snatched a tube of mace from her desk drawer, concealed it in her hand, and then walked along the front of the aisles, carefully looking down each one. She stopped before the last aisle. Slade stood near the end of the aisle holding a folder in his hand while browsing through it. She frowned with a disapproving glare.

"You said you'd wait for my supervisor," she announced with a soft hiss in her tone.

He glanced up briefly then looked back at the folder he flipped through and casually approached without looking up.

"I never said that," he stated simply. "You're doing your job, and I'm doing mine." He walked past her without even looking at her. "And please put that mace away. It would be a federal offense to use it on a federal agent."

He walked from the aisle while studying the contents of the folder. Jolynn stared after him with surprise then uncertainly followed him from a distance. Slade collapsed into the chair behind her desk and made himself comfortable. Jolynn glared at him, clearly annoyed as she folded her arms across her chest. The file room door was thrown open to reveal a tall, slender man in his early forties. Jolynn's boss, Paul McQueen, entered in a hurry, responding to her urgent phone call. McQueen was a distinguished looking man and mildly rugged in appearance with some gray along his temples in his otherwise dark hair.

Despite his imposing appearance, he wasn't much of a force to be reckoned with. Jolynn pegged him as a pushover, and the first time she'd met his wife, his pushover status was confirmed. McQueen's wife kept his manly parts tucked firmly in her purse. Jolynn respected him as a boss though, and she knew he'd take the hospital's privacy issues seriously. She hoped her boss would put this so-called federal agent in his place. McQueen looked at Jolynn with his mouth slightly opened then glared at Slade seeming at home comfortably seated behind the desk.

"May I help you?" McQueen demanded impatiently and asserted his male dominance.

Slade looked up with increased annoyance and huffed, dropping the file while dramatically throwing his arms in the air. "I certainly wish someone would."

As Slade stood and again flashed his badge, Jolynn attempted to take another look at it. The badge disappeared just as quickly as it had been produced, once again giving her no opportunity to verify its authenticity.

"Agent Slade, FBI," he announced while tucking his badge back into his inner jacket pocket. "I'm investigating a murder, and I need to look through several files."

"We have privacy laws here, Agent Slade," McQueen informed him. "I'm afraid you're going to need--"

"Your court order is already in the works," Slade gruffly announced as his eyes pierced through McQueen's eyes. "I could certainly wait until tomorrow and come back with that search warrant, if you'd prefer." His eyes narrowed slightly followed by a sly smirk. "That'll give me all afternoon to conduct a thorough background check on you, Mr. McQueen. Standard practice in cases like this. I'm sure you have nothing to hide."

McQueen suddenly fidgeted then looked at Jolynn with some surprise. She practically witnessed his spine shriveling up inside his back. He looked back at Slade and immediately appeared embarrassed by the situation, even managing a nervous laugh.

"There's no need to make you wait until tomorrow, Agent Slade. I certainly wouldn't want to inconvenience you," McQueen announced in a slightly higher pitch than normal. "Jolynn will get whatever you need."

Slade returned to the chair behind the desk and skimmed the open file before him. "It's nice to get a little cooperation from someone," Slade boldly remarked. He then muttered, "It's more than I've received so far."

McQueen appeared tense and immediately turned to Jolynn. "Why don't you get Agent Slade some coffee?"

Jolynn stared at McQueen with her mouth hanging open in utter surprise. She couldn't believe her boss was willing to kiss the man's ass just because he flashed what may or may not have been an official badge. Was it possible her wimp of a boss actually had something he feared the FBI discovering? McQueen couldn't possibly be that interesting. The more she thought about it, the angrier she became. She was all for helping law enforcement but the situation reeked of something foul.

"Black. Two sugar," Slade practically ordered without bothering to look up from his folder then brushed her off like a speck of dirt on his sleeve.

She glared at her boss. "Mr. McQueen--" Jolynn protested softly.

Certainly, he had to consider laws of confidentiality concerning patient files. He couldn't be that much of a pushover. McQueen glared his response and motioned her to leave. Maybe he did have something to hide after all. Perhaps the rumors of his wife having an affair were in fact true. Was he attempting to save face from some embarrassing find? Actually, she didn't care. It would all be on him for allowing a possible stranger access to classified files. She frowned her annoyance and headed for the door.

"I see why you keep her locked in the basement," Slade remarked while casually looking up at her boss. "Doesn't seem the type to play well with others."

Jolynn paused by the door and glared back at the man comfortably seated behind her desk. Neither man seemed to notice nor care that she was still within the room.

"You have to forgive Jolynn," McQueen informed Slade with an uneasy laugh. "She's a fine employee, but you're absolutely right. She doesn't work well with others."

Jolynn couldn't believe McQueen sold her out so easily. She gritted her teeth and left, slamming the door behind her. If they had forgotten she was still in the room, they certainly knew it at that moment. McQueen fidgeted and smiled timidly at Slade. It was obvious he knew she'd make him pay for his betrayal later.

Chapter Nine

Jolynn entered the records room and paused within the doorway to glare at the man behind her desk. She took a deep breath and reluctantly approached Slade with a Styrofoam cup of coffee. He appeared engrossed in the first file he'd found on his own. Naturally, McQueen was already gone, slipping out like a scolded dog with his tail firmly between his legs. Slade didn't bother looking up as she approached.

"And it better not find its way on my lap," he muttered under his breath.

Jolynn hesitated a moment, contemplating the comment as a challenge, then reluctantly set the cup on a small vacant spot on her desk. She hated to admit she'd given it serious consideration. Slade closed the file and tossed it across the cluttered desk. He placed a list on top of the file, took the cup of coffee, and casually leaned back while looking at her. Jolynn didn't take her eyes from him. If he was attempting to intimidate her with his stare, it wasn't working. She refused to look away or show any emotion. As she attempted to read his eyes, she almost felt him attempting to read hers.

"That's a list of the files I'll need to review," he announced in a moderately commanding tone then casually looked away. "Don't be all day about it."

His comment and tone were enough to cause her to twitch with anger. Had the cup of coffee still been in her hand, it almost certainly would have ended up in his lap. She controlled her hostility, thinking better of assaulting a federal agent.

Slade casually sipped his coffee then made a face and looked at the cup. "That's godawful! Is there anything not bitter around here?"

She held back her comment, snatched the list from the desk, and stormed across the file room. As soon as her back was turned, Slade glanced up from his cup of coffee and watched her with more than a passing interest.

✝

Jolynn remained out of sight of her desk and the despicable Agent Slade while gathering several files he'd requested on the lengthy list. She'd only been out of his sight for a few minutes when she heard what sounded like her desk drawer closing. Jolynn appeared curious as to what he was doing back at her desk. She approached the aisle opening with several files in her arms and looked across the room to where Slade remained sitting behind her desk. He sat casually reclined in her chair with his eyes closed and his feet propped and crossed on the desktop. She knew what she had heard. She was positive he had been routing through her desk, although she had no idea what he would be looking for.

Perhaps he was just nosy, but she wasn't going to tolerate any bullshit from the arrogant man no matter what his position. Jolynn approached the desk and, with added vigor, dropped the files on top. She had been hoping they'd make a loud enough crack to startle the resting man, but they didn't make nearly as much noise as she would've liked. Slade opened his eyes, allowing his feet to drop to the floor as he snatched the first file. Without a word or acknowledgement, he flipped through the file. She sneered, even though he didn't see it, and continued on her mission to collect more files for the pompous idiot.

✝

*L*ater. Jolynn entered the file room carrying another cup of coffee for Slade. Her mood hadn't improved any as she placed the second cup of black coffee on the desk near Slade. She glanced at the file he held open before him, only getting a peek before he waved her off like an annoying fly. Jolynn sneered and walked away. He was an insufferable man, which explained his lack of a wedding band. Despite being undeniably handsome, no woman in her right mind would subject herself to someone like Slade. She heaved herself onto a two-drawer filing cabinet not far from the desk and watched him with annoyance. If it was his intent to annoy her and belittle her, she wasn't going to let him succeed. In fact, she intended to render her own form of intimidation by watching his every move. She didn't trust him, federal agent or not, and she intended to make her feelings known.

It seemed as if a lifetime had passed before McQueen finally returned to the records room. Jolynn remained sitting on the filing cabinet with her back to the wall, bored and just about falling asleep. When McQueen glanced at her where she sat, she glared her annoyance with him. McQueen attempted to ignore the look he received and focused his attention on the agent sitting behind her desk. Slade continued to skim through the files. McQueen appeared edgy, but Jolynn doubted he'd confront Slade about his business. Jolynn was rapidly losing respect for her boss.

"Are you finding everything you need, Agent Slade?" McQueen finally asked, forcing a smile.

Slade didn't bother looking up. "Hmm?" he muttered with disinterest then seemed to realize he'd been asked a question. "Oh, yes--"

McQueen appeared uneasy, briefly glanced at Jolynn, and then looked back at Slade with a tiny smile as he perfected his ass kissing technique. "If there's anything else you need, anything at all, just ask."

Jolynn again glared at McQueen. He was unbelievable. She couldn't believe he was just letting this man route through any file he wanted without being asked as much as 'why'. McQueen caught her glare and quickly hurried from the room to avoid her wrath. Slade finally tossed down the last folder and stood with some stiffness. Jolynn sprang from her filing cabinet and watched him with anticipation. He approached the door near where she stood and paused before her.

"Your cooperation was greatly appreciated." He extended his card. "If anyone else comes around looking for those files, call me immediately."

Jolynn eyed the card then took it from him by the very edge, as if it was contaminated.

"Good afternoon, Ms. Raynard."

He left the records room leaving Jolynn baffled and bewildered. It wasn't as if she told him her last name nor was it anywhere on top of her desk for him to have seen it. Once she was sure he was gone, she hurried to her desk and pulled open each drawer, searching for anything that might be missing or out of place. She then removed her purse. It was zipped all the way shut, which wasn't how she had left it. While at work, her purse was almost always partially unzipped for easy access to her cell phone and, more importantly, her stun gun.

Chapter Ten

Jolynn sat behind her desk with her cell phone to her ear while the contents of her purse lay scattered across the desk. She didn't carry much in her purse, but it was enough to leave quite a mess, making her wonder why she even needed half the contents before her. She was still irritated while expressing her hostility to her friend on the other end of her call.

"I'm telling you, Gillian, the bastard went through my purse," Jolynn snarled while inspecting the contents of her wallet. "He was checking out my driver's license."

"Yeah, like the FBI just wanted to snoop through your purse. Trust me; if he was with the FBI, he already knows who you are. He doesn't need to look through your purse to figure that out," Gillian scoffed from the other end. "You're overreacting, as usual. Your imagination never stops."

Jolynn leaned forward on her desk and clutched the cell phone with mild agitation. She continued to scan the contents of her purse and shook her head.

"I'm telling you, he was a very suspicious character," Jolynn protested then frowned. "I'm willing to bet he wasn't a fed at all.

43

And that's another thing. I looked through the files he requested. I found that to be awfully suspicious also. They were all young women. Women our age."

"Maybe he's hard up for a date," her friend teased through the phone.

"That's not funny," Jolynn snarled, finding it difficult to relax. "He knew my last name, which means he looked at my driver's license. That means he may also know where we live. What if this guy is some sort of stalker or serial killer?"

"Stop, you're creeping me out," Gillian remarked in a dreary, unconcerned tone. "If you're so concerned, why don't you call the FBI and check on his story?"

Jolynn sat back in her chair and stared at the ceiling while exhaling deeply. "They probably wouldn't tell me either way," she muttered.

"Put your imagination to rest for a while," Gillian finally announced then became enthusiastic. "It's Friday and nearly quitting time. Why don't I meet you at Jerry's Tavern for a few drinks? It'll be fun. You sound like you need to unwind."

"Nice try. You played hooky today," Jolynn reminded her friend in a scolding tone. "You can't go out to a bar this evening. You're grounded."

"I'm bored," she whined.

"All the more reason why you should've gone to work," Jolynn insisted then considered the comment. "*I* should've stayed home."

"Was he at least cute?"

Jolynn refrained from rolling her eyes at the question. It was so typical of Gillian to ask such a thing. As if a creepy guy being good looking would make a difference.

"Who could tell," she muttered. "I couldn't get past his charming personality. I love being treated like a dog. It turns me on."

"Ah, ha," Gillian cried out through the phone. "That proves he was a real fed. Who else would treat others with disrespect and like a subhuman?"

"There was just something very suspicious about him," Jolynn remarked with concern. "Promise you'll keep the doors locked until I get home."

"Yeah, sure," Gillian replied with a bored sigh. "I'll pick up a movie. We can have a girls' Friday night." She then giggled softly. "Unless you're going out with Dan."

"Please--"

"Dan's not so bad. At least he's cute. You really need to date more," Gillian insisted. "I'm starting to worry you might find me attractive."

"You're so funny," Jolynn scoffed with irritation. "If I remember correctly, you shot Dan down several times when he asked you out."

"I didn't shoot him down," Gillian protested. "I let him down easy."

"You let him have it with both barrels of a twelve gauge shotgun," Jolynn scoffed.

"I've never rejected any guy that harshly," Gillian protested through the phone.

"Oh, please!"

There was a brief pause. "Fine, I rejected the guy, but that's me. You can't afford to be quite so picky with guys," Gillian informed her.

"Thanks, Gillian," Jolynn scoffed with annoyance. "I wasn't sure I could feel any worse today. So glad I could count on you to accept the challenge."

"Okay, that didn't come out the way I meant it," Gillian protested.

"Sure it didn't," Jolynn muttered and leaned back in the chair behind her desk.

Gillian laughed softly. "You take everything so literally." There was a brief pause. "Don't worry about me. Nothing happens in this hick town. I'll talk to you later." Gillian disconnected the call.

Jolynn shook her head then set her cell phone down with a disgusted groan. She leaned forward on the desk and held her head in both hands.

"I wish she'd get married already."

✝

Gillian cast the cordless phone aside from where she was comfortably spread out on the loveseat. She lazily rolled over the back of the loveseat, made it to her feet, and shuffled down the hallway, not once bothering to check that the apartment door was locked. She was still in her satin nightgown with matching robe despite it being nearly three o'clock in the afternoon. Gillian shuffled into the bathroom, leaving the door open, and turned on the water for her bubble bath. As the tub filled, she left the bathroom and entered her bedroom. Her bedroom was frilly and welcoming to potential gentleman callers. Gillian enjoyed entertaining, although she usually only brought thoroughly vetted boyfriends into her shared apartment. Jolynn was opposed to unfamiliar men spending the night. Although Gillian would never admit it, she wasn't nearly as promiscuous as she let Jolynn think she was.

She grabbed a clean pair of panties and matching, lacy bra, which somehow indicated she was considering going out that night against Jolynn's suggestion. Gillian carried her undergarments toward the bathroom and suddenly stopped in the hallway. The tub water was no longer running. Gillian tensed and looked around with obvious horror. She quickly and quietly ran back down the hall and hurried into Jolynn's room. She picked up the bedside phone and dialed 911. Before she even finished dialing, she heard a busy tone, indicating the living room phone had been left on, but she had definitely turned it off. Gillian looked around Jolynn's moderately bland, gender-neutral bedroom and ran for the bed headboard. She removed a baseball bat and clung to it with sweaty palms.

Gillian slowly entered the hallway while clinging to the baseball bat and approached the partially open bathroom door. She looked beyond the door to the living room and sweet freedom but something caused her to stop. She heard the water splashing slightly within the tub. She appeared baffled then slowly pushed the door open the rest of the way while keeping a secure grip on the baseball bat. As the door opened, she saw Larry and his bare muscular chest as he lounged in the bubble-filled bathtub. She lowered the bat while staring at the naked man as her mouth hung open.

"Larry! What the--?"

He saw her and grinned boyishly with white teeth and sexy dimples. "When you called in sick, I thought you could use the company," he announced cheerfully. "I was thinking wine, but then I saw the romantic tub for two--"

"Get out," she cried out while jumping in place.

"Oh, come on," he announced while making a pouting face for her benefit. "Don't I get a little sympathy sex for the romantic gesture?"

"Get out! Get out! Get out!" she screamed while swinging the bat, striking the side of the tub for added effect.

Larry jumped several times to the sound of the bat hitting the fiberglass tub. He held his hands in the air defensively.

"Okay, okay," he cried out while attempting to shield his face then relaxed as she loosened her grip on the bat. "What the hell is wrong with you?" he scoffed in a low tone. "I'd say you need to get laid, but we both know that already happened."

Gillian cried out with hostility, snatched the showerhead from its holder, and turned on the cold water. She immediately sprayed Larry in the face with the cold water. He screamed while blocking his face as he jumped out of the tub. She turned the cold water from the showerhead to his bubble-covered crotch, freezing him where it counted most. He continued to scream, scooped up his clothes, and ran from the bathroom. Gillian cast the showerhead aside and chased after him with the baseball bat.

Chapter Eleven

McQueen poked his head through the door into the medical records and glanced around with a nervous look. Jolynn cast a glare at him from where she sat behind her desk. Her boss was such a disappointment to her. She couldn't believe he'd allow Agent Slade berate her as he did let alone give him access to confidential client information. She blamed him for whatever consequences would arise from Agent Slade's visit. The contents of Jolynn's purse still lay scattered across the desktop. She wasn't giving up so easily on the invasion of her own privacy either.

"Is he gone?" McQueen whispered to her.

"Yeah," she muttered with disgust. "He's gone."

Jolynn had to bite her tongue to keep from cursing out her boss. McQueen entered and appeared relieved by the news. Jolynn glared at him with disgust as he approached her desk as if nothing ever happened.

"You're such a wuss, Paul," Jolynn snarled. "Just leave me hanging in the breeze--"

"Hey, I just bought a very cute sports car," McQueen informed her. "I don't need the feds crawling up my ass with a microscope."

"If he even was a fed."

"He had a badge," McQueen insisted.

"Probably from a gumball machine," she muttered.

McQueen sat on the edge of her desk and stared at her. "He was a fed all right," he announced without hesitation. "No one can fake a superior attitude like that."

"As long as you think so," she snapped and avoided looking at him in an attempt to control her hostility. "Just know that I'm not taking any responsibility for allowing him access to all those files. It's all on you."

McQueen picked up the list of names from her desk and studied it. Jolynn replaced items lying on the desk to her purse with disgust.

"What do you suppose he was looking for?"

Jolynn focused her attention on her purse. "Lipstick, perhaps," she muttered.

"What?"

"He went through my purse," she boldly announced with irritation while continuing to toss items back into her purse. "I'm convinced of that."

Her boss cocked his head to the side and appeared surprised. "Why would he look through your purse?"

"I don't know, but he knew my last name," she insisted and cast a look at her boss.

"I certainly didn't tell him your last name," McQueen informed her. "I didn't even want him knowing mine." He returned to the list of names and suddenly appeared curious. "That's weird. All these women are around the same age."

"Yeah, I noticed," she muttered.

"Very strange. Almost all of these women went to school with my niece," McQueen informed her and remained suspicious about the list. "I recognize most of the girls on here." He glanced at her with a strange look and raised his brow in question. "Why do you suppose he wanted birth records and history on these particular women?"

"I don't know," Jolynn replied with a defeated sigh. "But I'm not going to think about it until Monday. I've had enough of this day."

Her boss set the paper down on her desk and stood. "At least your name wasn't on that list," he announced. "After all, you're in that age group." He then eyed her with a curious look. "You went to school with my niece, didn't you?"

"No," Jolynn replied with little emotion. "I didn't move here until after I graduated high school."

"Well, whatever the reason for his interest in those files, you weren't on his list, so I assume you're safe," McQueen teased and flashed a grin. "Let's not worry about it until Monday. I'll make some calls then and see if we can figure out what he wanted with girls from those two graduating classes."

His words finally sank in. Taking into consideration that Agent Slade mentioned a murder investigation, Jolynn felt slightly insecure and rubbed her slightly chilled arms.

"Yeah, sure," she replied with less enthusiasm, now lacking her earlier confidence.

"I'm heading out," he announced with enthusiasm. "I'll see you Monday."

She watched her boss leave and then sank into thought. She shook the thoughts from her head, grabbed a stack of files remaining on her desk, and headed for the last aisle to return them. Jolynn was only away from her desk a few minutes when she heard someone within the records room. She hadn't heard the door open, which was moderately alarming. She could hear the distinct sound of someone typing on her computer. Jolynn held back her gasp, gently set her files down, and quickly but quietly hurried to the end of the aisle. She cast a look at her desk. To her surprise, there was no one there. The chair turned slightly, as if someone had just moved from it. Jolynn withheld her gasp while fumbling in her pocket for the small container of mace. She silently walked toward her desk while looking down each aisle she passed. As Jolynn approached the aisle closest to her desk, Dan emerged from the aisle and nearly collided with her. Both screamed and jumped.

"Damn it," Dan cried out while clutching his chest. "You scared me!"

"What the hell are you doing sneaking around down here?" she demanded as she ran trembling fingers through her hair.

"I wasn't sneaking," Dan protested. "You were supposed to be gone half an hour ago. One of the nurses requested a file." He was obviously nerve racked as well. "Why are you still here? It's Friday. No one stays late on a Friday."

"I had a few things to clean up," she replied, finally controlling her rapidly racing pulse. "You should have known I was still here when you noticed the door was unlocked. Next time, announce yourself."

"You're jumpy," Dan scoffed then offered a teasing grin. "Afraid of the big bad fed?"

She folded her arms across her chest defensively. "Is McQueen telling everyone about my day?" she demanded then

50

groaned. "No, I'm not afraid of feds. I just didn't care for the one I'd met." She gestured with annoyance. "Take your file and go. I need to lock up. It's late, and I'm tired."

"Cranky too," Dan muttered and eyed her. "Guess I should be glad you wouldn't go out with me. Get more than I'd bargained for."

"Goodbye, Dan."

✝

Jolynn left the hospital only a few minutes later and walked along the sidewalk past the parking lot. Since she only lived a few blocks from the hospital, she usually walked to work. It made sense, especially on nice days. She passed several people entering the hospital. Something caused her to stop and look around. She had a strange feeling she was being watched. When she didn't see anything unusual, Jolynn continued in the direction of her apartment but she couldn't shake the feeling and it left her slightly rattled. A black van pulled out from the parking lot after she'd passed and immediately parked along the curb. As Jolynn walked around the corner, the van pulled away from the curb and drove behind her until the next intersection. She suspiciously looked back at the van then watched it make the turn and drive away.

Chapter Twelve

Gillian grabbed her purse as she headed for the apartment door, stuffing her credit card down the front of her shirt. It was an odd habit she'd gotten into after her purse had been stolen once. She was dressed casually in jeans and a sweatshirt with her hair carelessly thrown into a ponytail. She unlocked and barely opened the door then hesitated with an afterthought.

"Keys," she muttered and opened her purse. It would be asking too much for the keys to be right on top and in plain sight. She groaned softly and dug through her excessively large purse with a look of frustration.

"I can never find my damned keys," she snapped then groaned while continuing her quest to find them. "I need a smaller purse."

Gillian produced her ring of only four keys with an equal number of decorative keychains, making the ring seem larger than necessary. Before she could leave, the phone rang. She groaned softly, only considered not answering it briefly, and then approached the cordless phone on the table alongside the loveseat. She picked up the receiver without looking at the caller ID.

"Hello?" There was no response. She immediately became frustrated. "Hello? Larry?" she almost demanded, her good mood fading. "Go to hell." Gillian disconnected the call and tossed the cordless phone with disgust onto the loveseat. "Jerk."

Gillian stormed toward the open door and hurried from the apartment, slamming the door behind her without bothering to lock it. She trotted down the carpeted stairs with a lively step, attempting to return to her good mood, and hummed softly to herself. She heard the faint thud of footfalls on the stairs above her. Gillian glanced back but wasn't too concerned when she didn't see anyone behind her. She emerged from the back of the building, which brought her to the small parking lot used for tenant parking only. She swung her large keyring without a care as she approached her silver car parked alongside an unmarked white van. Someone else also left the building through the back door and headed into the lot as well. Gillian unlocked her car door then heard the person just leaving the building approaching her from behind. It no longer seemed to be a coincidence. Gillian groaned with limited patience and spun around.

"Okay, Larry, stop following--"

Gillian's expression suddenly dropped. A black, gloved hand grabbed her by the throat and slammed her against her car door, cracking the window from the force of the blow. She was temporarily dazed as her keys fell to the pavement. Gillian suddenly came back to her senses, gasped at the tight hand on her throat, and frantically fought the hand that prevented her from breathing. A cloth reeking of chemicals was firmly held over her nose and mouth. She clutched and clawed at the gloved hand holding the rag. As she gasped for air, she inhaled the chemicals soaked into the cloth. Despite her effort to remove either gloved hand, she became weak and slowly drifted into unconsciousness.

†

Jolynn approached the front of her apartment building and stopped before the main entrance to fumble with her keys. She suddenly clutched her head and the exploding pressure in her temples almost paralyzed her. Her keys fell from her hand and struck the mat before the door. She saw a flash of an unconscious Gillian being thrown into the back of a white van. Jolynn gasped while releasing her head and ran around the side of the building to the back parking lot. As she ran into the parking lot, she saw a white van pulling out at the same time. Jolynn ran across the parking lot to where Gillian's car was parked. Her large keyring was on the ground next to the driver's side door with the cracked window containing a tiny trace of blood. Jolynn looked across the lot as the van careened down the road prepared to vanish from her sight. She fumbled with the keys, threw open the unlocked car door, and jumped inside. Gillian's silver car peeled out of the parking space, slid into a turn, and jetted forward toward the main road after the van.

Gillian's car chased after the white van to the first stop light as it turned yellow. The van ran the yellow light. Jolynn didn't stop despite the light turning red. Several cars swerved to avoid hitting her in the intersection. Her car spun around as she slammed on the brakes to avoid a head-on collision with another car. Her route was now blocked by stopped cars and their drivers who screamed profanities through open windows at her. Jolynn looked around, but it was too late. The white van was gone.

Chapter Thirteen

The abandoned train station waiting area was dimly lit from the little light peeking through dirty, broken windowpanes. There were rows of benches, some rotted and broken, within the dirty, dingy waiting area. A few of the stained glass windows were intact, although most were either cracked or broken. Old, outdated billboards, coated thick with dirt, were on display along the walls. A train whistle was heard in the near distance. Beth lay awake on a sturdy, old bench. She had duct tape across her mouth and also binding her wrists and ankles. She struggled against her bindings while gasping beneath the duct tape covering her mouth keeping her silent. The old remains of blood and mostly burned candles were seen along the floor in a circular pattern surrounding her.

After several attempts, Beth frantically pulled herself into a sitting position. A door opened with a distinctive echo from somewhere within the old station. Beth managed to pull herself to her feet and hopped across the station to the nearby restrooms. She pushed herself into the door, opening it with her body, and disappeared inside.

The old-fashioned, multi-stall bathroom was in severe disrepair. The dirty sinks were cracked and stained. The mirrors were mostly shattered and the stall doors were falling off their hinges. Beth moved alongside the now closed door. She could hear movement from the waiting area followed by a crash. Beth hopped to the far corner near an old, broken window. She hid within the back corner just out of sight of the door and listened to the sounds from the waiting area. Someone slung and kicked objects around within the next room. Her kidnapper discovered she was missing and wasn't very happy. Beth shut her eyes and held her breath. Hiding was futile. It was almost stupid to think he wouldn't find her. The bathroom would obviously be the first place he'd look.

The sound of boys laughing and skateboarding was heard just beyond the window. Beth's eyes lit up to the sound. She managed to look out the dirty, broken window. Three younger teenage boys skateboarded around the old parking lot toward the rear of the abandoned train station. Beth frantically rubbed her face against the window frame, slowly peeling back the duct tape. The bathroom door was thrown open with a loud bang. Beth worked faster to remove the tape from her mouth. The tape was only halfway off, but it was enough. She could almost feel a shadow looming over her from behind, but she refused to turn around. She didn't want to see him coming.

"Help," she screamed through the broken pane in the window.

Beth was violently pulled away from the window and thrown across the bathroom. She struck the floor and slid a foot or two. Just outside the train station, one of the boys stopped his skateboard and looked around with bewilderment. He glanced at the backside of the building and stared a moment. The other two boys continued to skateboard away. The remaining boy eyed the broken bathroom window and appeared curious. When nothing moved and no other sound followed, he shrugged and followed after his friends.

†

*B*eth slowly opened her eyes and stared at a close-up of the dirty bathroom tile. As disorientation passed, she looked around and realized she was still within the train station bathroom, although now she was on the floor near the door. The tape was once again across her mouth, although it wasn't sticking in place as well as it had. She heard a faint male voice beyond the bathroom possibly coming from the main waiting area. She pulled herself into a sitting position, scooted onto her backside until her back was to the door, and worked on opening the door with her hands still tied behind her back. With some effort, she opened the door enough to work herself through the opening. She looked across the massive train station and saw the thirteen-year-old boy with his skateboard standing in the far doorway. He looked around then spotted the burning candles surrounding the old bench.

"Hello?" he called out. "Is there someone here?"

Beth attempted to muffle a scream, but nothing came out. The young boy, appearing curious yet apprehensive, headed across the station toward the burning candles. A shadow loomed over him. He suddenly gasped and spun around, coming face-to-face with a homeless man. The homeless man wore tattered, grimy clothing. His moderately long hair and scruffy beard were tangled and filthy as was the rest of his face. Despite his haggard condition, the homeless man was sturdy looking and possibly only in his late thirties. The boy cried out and jumped back with surprise.

"You shouldn't be here," the homeless man growled at the boy.

"I, uh, thought I heard someone calling for help," the boy fumbled over his words.

"I know what you were doing," the homeless man snarled back and gave a nod to the candles. "Burn the place down without half trying. You shouldn't be here. This is not the sort of place for a little boy. Now go on. Get out of here."

The boy gasped with fright, turned, and ran from the station with his skateboard tucked under his arm. The homeless man shook his head then headed toward the burning candles across the main station. He slowed when he saw the symbol surrounding the bench then looked around. His eyes met Beth's where she still sat in the bathroom doorway. She gasped with horror beneath the tape covering her mouth and attempted to pull herself to her feet. The homeless man stared only a moment longer then ran for her. Beth again attempted to scream, but he was on top of her within seconds. The homeless man lowered himself to one knee before her, stared at her with surprise, and then pulled the tape from her mouth.

"What happened?" he suddenly demanded and searched her eyes. "Are you okay?"

Beth stared at him only a moment before realizing he wasn't the man who'd abducted her. "Untie me," she cried out softly. "We need to get out of here before he comes back."

The homeless man barely let the words sink in before removing a switchblade knife from his pocket. He slashed the duct tape binding her ankles then moved for her wrists bound behind her. Beth looked up as he paritally cut the duct tape and saw her abductor standing over them. It was her first real look at the man who kidnapped her. He was average height and wore a tattered, old trench coat to conceal his frame size. None of that mattered to Beth. All she saw was the frightening, full head zombie clown mask he wore to conceal his identity. She screamed a warning. The homeless man spun on his knees as the dagger was thrust downward, striking his shoulder rather than his back as intended.

As the Pen Pal pulled the dagger free for another attempt, the homeless man sprang to his feet and lunged for him with his switchblade. Beth cried out while fighting the partially cut duct tape still binding her wrists. As she struggled to free herself, she helplessly watched the two men tangled together on the floor slashing at each other with their knives. The homeless man seemed determined and was holding his own against the frightening attacker. For a moment, Beth was filled with hope of a rescue. Both men sprang to their feet.

Rather than simply take off and save himself, the homeless man accepted the challenge of his masked attacker. The Pen Pal slammed the man into the nearby wall despite taking a poke from the switchblade to his side. He thrust his dagger into the homeless man's throat, catching him by surprise. As he pulled the dagger free, blood poured from the man's neck. The homeless man slowly sank to the floor, a pool of blood swiftly collecting around him. Beth stared at the dead man who had risked his life to save hers and sobbed softly for both their sakes.

Chapter Fourteen

Jolynn paced the small, cluttered sheriff's office encased in a wall of glass. Several police officers could be seen in the bullpen through the glass divider as they sifted through mounds of paperwork. They seemed unusually busy for such a small town. Sheriff Gruber entered his office and immediately eyed Jolynn with a look she'd seen too often from others and had grown to dread. It was that look of disbelief or, on rarer occasions, a possible question of her sanity. He shut the door behind him and collapsed into the old, creaking chair behind his desk.

"Are you calm now?" he asked in a relaxed tone although his piercing eyes contained doubt.

He barely made himself comfortable when Jolynn lunged forward and hovered over his desk, silently answering his question. She knew she wasn't winning any points with the dense, country sheriff, but there wasn't a moment to waste, and his men had wasted enough of her time already.

"What's with you people?" she demanded, unable to follow through with the calm tone she had practiced in her head. "My roommate's been kidnapped and you make me wait an hour before even talking to me."

"She's only been gone two hours," Gruber remarked firmly as his eyes burned into hers. "That's hardly a missing person. You, on the other hand, came in here like a mad woman."

Jolynn held Gillian's keys and gave them a vigorous shake. "I found these next to her car," she insisted. "She was taken away in a white van. I saw it leave. I chased after them."

"And you witnessed her being thrown into this van?" Gruber demanded.

Jolynn hesitated and considered her answer carefully. "I saw the van speed away."

He groaned softly as he leaned forward, pretending to route through the clutter of papers on his desk. Was he attempting to convince her how busy he was?

"Do you know how many missing persons' reports I've had this afternoon? Twenty. Twenty missing persons' reports in the last few hours, each family member more animated than the last. That's in addition to the twelve from last night and the six from this morning. It seems as if everyone who watched the news last night has gone into paranoid mode." He fiddled with the pen on his desk. "Nearly thirty boogie man sightings today alone," he muttered under his breath then returned his attention to Jolynn while sighing deeply. "In almost every missing persons' case, each of the young ladies returned home a few hours later or the following morning, hungover and looking like hell."

"I'm telling you, Sheriff," she snapped hotly. "This is different."

"I've been hearing that all day. It's like an epidemic out there," he muttered then eyed her with disbelief. "Although you're by far the most edgy one." He drew a deep breath and sighed softly as he rubbed his eyes. "We'll fill out the paperwork and put out a report on your friend, if it'll get you out of my office," he announced, finally giving in.

"You need to send someone out to look at the parking lot," Jolynn insisted. "There may be clues. DNA."

"And we'll do that," he informed her then briefly hesitated, "if she's not back in twenty-four hours."

"She could be dead in twenty-four hours," she exploded while nearly lunging across the desk.

Gruber abruptly stood, lacking patience, and leaned across the desk to greet her with a stern glare. "You need to calm down, young lady," he snarled lowly without taking his eyes off hers. "We don't have the manpower to send someone out every time a girl runs off for an afternoon delight with her boyfriend."

His words cut through Jolynn, stinging from the sexist remark that unfortunately pretty much described Gillian's behavior. "There is no boyfriend." It wasn't a lie. Larry was a drunken case of bad judgement. "I'm telling you, she was kidnapped!" Her temper was rising quickly and to unhealthy levels. "Why the hell won't you listen to what I'm saying? She didn't run away, she was going to get a movie, that's all!"

Gruber stood straight, attempting his best intimidating pose after her sudden outburst. "You either need to stop using that tone or go home," he announced while pointing an angry, stubby finger at her. "I'm very close to throwing you into a cell until you cool down."

Jolynn made a half-hearted attempt to control her emotions. She drew a deep breath but couldn't keep her body from twitching with adrenaline.

"Send someone out to my apartment," she announced in the calmest voice she could manage, although her eyes were piercing into his without mercy. "I'll show you the van's tire marks. The longer you wait, the greater the chance she'll be dead." She held her breath a moment to keep her emotions in check. "Can I make it any clearer?"

"Yes, you can fill out the paperwork," he replied. "We'll report it, and the detectives will look into it tomorrow if she's not back."

Jolynn grew frustrated by the constant runaround the entire police department had been giving her. She groaned softly and ran her fingers through her hair a little harder than necessary to maintain her calm demeanor. An image suddenly flashed in her mind, bringing about a sharp, stabbing pain within her temples. Jolynn held her temples and nearly doubled over from the vision in her mind. She saw Gillian lying on the floor in a darkened room with her hands and feet bound with duct tape. Gillian slowly came to, although disoriented, and looked around. She was lying in a symbol drawn in blood with candles surrounding her.

At key points of the symbol, there were bloody, internal organs positioned around her. Gillian attempted to scream through the duct tape across her mouth. Jolynn slipped back into reality while releasing a painful gasp. Her expression suddenly dropped as her entire body trembled from the vision. She leaped for the desk with renewed urgency and fear, practically lunging for the sheriff as he quizzically watched her strange behavior just a moment earlier.

"He's going to kill her," she cried out. "You have to do something!"

Gruber jumped back with surprise by her sudden, violent outburst then became angry. He stormed around the desk, walked directly up to her, and pointed at the door. Jolynn took a quick, startled step away from him with a look of uncontrolled stress and fear.

"That's enough," Gruber growled. "Get out of my office, or I'll have you arrested!"

Jolynn backed up another step and started sobbing from the horrifying vision. "He's going to kill her!"

Gruber grabbed Jolynn's arm with limited sympathy. "I want you out now!"

Jolynn jerked harshly from his hand holding her arm and pulled away from him with a terrified scream as if he was hurting her.

"Don't touch me!"

She clutched her arm and backed away from him with a wild, unpredictable look somewhere between fear and rage. She was completely hysterical now. Gruber signaled through the glass partition. Deputy Hunt and another officer rushed for the office to assist.

"Do something you fucking bastard," she cried out. "Help her, goddamn it!"

Both officers ran into the office and grabbed Jolynn by the arms. She screamed and attempted to pull from them as if she were being tortured. Images of Deputy Hunt arresting criminals and tending to accident scenes flashed through her mind like a tidal wave. Some were brutal and horrifying. Her head pounded with each image causing her to cry out in agony.

"No! Don't touch me!"

She violently struggled against the police officers then kicked Deputy Hunt in the groin. He dropped to his knees, releasing her. Gruber leaped for her. She punched him harshly in the mouth, casting him back several steps with the wild, hard hit. The second officer tackled her to the floor.

Chapter Fifteen

Jolynn sat quietly in the empty cell by herself with her hands cuffed behind her back. She was reclined casually against the wall with her eyes closed and the appearance of someone who had been heavily sedated. The few female prisoners being held in the nearby cells suddenly yelled sexual remarks and whistled. Jolynn heard Deputy Hunt's voice within the lockup corridor as he approached while talking to someone.

"They're sending someone over from the state hospital to evaluate her," Deputy Hunt informed the man walking alongside him. "Trust me; you don't want to go in there."

"I think I'll survive," the familiar male voice replied while getting closer.

Jolynn opened her eyes to the familiar voice and looked at the men approaching her cell. Agent Slade stood alongside Deputy Hunt, facing him just outside the cell. Although skeptical, Deputy Hunt unlocked the door, allowing Slade to enter, then immediately locked the door behind him. The deputy stood by the door as if awaiting some freak force of nature to occur. Slade placed his hands in his pockets and calmly looked back at Hunt.

"That'll be all for now."

Deputy Hunt reluctantly left them. Jolynn couldn't deny she was curious by Slade's presence, but she was too doped to react. She looked away without expression. Slade paced the cell while studying her then paused several feet away.

"Four counts of battery," he casually announced as he folded his arms across his chest. "Striking an officer." He attempted to hide a slightly amused smirk. "The sheriff no less." His look immediately returned to something more serious. "Misconduct. The list goes on."

Jolynn didn't bother looking at him. She had no strength to fight him physically or verbally. "Fuck off."

"I see the sedation they gave you didn't affect your charming personality."

Slade sat on the bunk across from her and clasped his hands together between his knees. He studied her a long moment even though she refused to look at him.

"Would you care to discuss what happened?" he asked while tilting his head.

"No."

"Okay, then I'll report Gruber's version." He again stood and paced. "You reported a missing person, not really missing yet, refused to fill out the paperwork, became violent, and attacked Gruber and two other officers," Slade announced then looked at her. "How am I doing so far?"

Jolynn shut her eyes and could almost feel herself fading off to sleep. "You're a prick."

Slade stopped pacing and stared at her. "That may be true, but I'd also like to find out what happened to your friend," he informed her then raised his brows while studying her. "Wouldn't you?"

She barely opened her eyes. Somehow, in her doped state, she couldn't help notice his commanding presence and handsome features. Obviously, the drugs were to blame.

"The police won't do anything for twenty-four hours," she remarked while struggling to wake herself. "Why would the FBI care?"

Slade sat on the cot alongside her. She managed to eye him as her body twitched. Unfortunately, she could only manage an untrusting look, being too sedated to react.

"Because I'm looking for a killer," Slade informed her. "If he has your friend, we don't have much time."

Jolynn stared at him a moment. Inside she was reacting, but she was unable to relay it physically due to the heavy sedation. Her eyes shut and her head fell back against the wall.

"What do you want to know?"

"Would you say your friend is between twenty and twenty-four, reddish hair, over five-foot-four and fairly attractive?" Slade asked.

She suddenly looked at him with concern and struggled to keep her eyes open. "Yes."

"How can you be sure she was kidnapped?" he asked, raising a curious brow. "Did you witness it?"

"No."

"Then how do you know?"

Her eyes once more shut involuntarily. "You couldn't possibly understand."

Slade frowned and shook his head. "You're absolutely no use to me when you're this doped up," he scoffed then approached the door. "Guard!"

Deputy Hunt approached and without hesitation unlocked the door for Slade. He straightened proudly while staring at the young officer.

"I want all the charges dropped and the young woman turned over into my custody," Slade commanded.

Deputy Hunt appeared stunned by the order. "I can't do that."

"Then get someone who can." He extended his hand to the officer. "The handcuff keys."

The deputy reluctantly handed him the handcuff keys. Slade returned to where Jolynn remained on the cot. Deputy Hunt locked the door behind him then hurried away. As Slade approached, Jolynn slowly moved away from the wall with a look of concern and possible paranoia.

"Don't touch me," she announced gruffly in a tone that was somewhere between fear and hostility.

He snorted a soft laugh, almost amused by her threat. "I wouldn't dream of it."

Slade unlocked the handcuffs from her wrists and tossed them onto the cot.

"We have a lot to discuss and very little time for explanations," he informed her. "I'll get you out of here and all the charges dropped. In exchange, you tell me everything I want to know."

She stared at him a moment before allowing her head to fall into her hand. Slade drew a deep breath and placed his hands in his pockets.

"I'll take that as acceptance to my terms," he boldly announced.

Chapter Sixteen

The small, out-of-the-way diner was the only place open that late at night. An old, tired waitress tended to her few patrons, which consisted of a scruffy looking man in tattered, dirty clothes, two exhausted women who were quite possibly prostitutes, and the fashionable Slade with his weary looking companion. Jolynn slouched over her cup of coffee as if she'd fall asleep at any moment. Anyone assessing her story might peg her for a drug addict. From their corner booth, Slade signaled the tired waitress for another refill. The unenthusiastic waitress brought them their breakfast and refreshed their coffee. It was possibly the worst coffee Jolynn had ever tasted, but she wasn't really much of a coffee drinker. She eyed the plate of scrambled eggs, bacon, and toast before her then cast a look through droopy eyes at Slade.

"I told you, I'm not hungry."

"And I told you that eating would help dilute the effects of the sedation," he interjected without care. "Now eat. Gillian's counting on us."

Jolynn allowed her head to fall weakly into her hands, sniffing while fighting back her tears. She had a thousand thoughts racing through her mind, but she couldn't organize any of them. Her best friend was in trouble and this man seemed to be the only one who believed her and was willing to help, yet she couldn't push past the sedation to ask the questions she needed to ask. The dark clouds in her mind finally parted, allowing a few lucid thoughts through. She lowered her hands and looked at him, able to focus on him for the first time.

"Who is this guy?"

"It's better if I didn't disclose that information," he replied without looking at her and concentrated on his breakfast platter. "You really don't want details." Slade devoured his eggs as if he'd been starving. He only briefly glanced at her between mouthfuls. "Tell me how you can be so certain she was abducted and not on a weekend rendezvous with some guy."

Jolynn clutched her head and her stomach. "I don't feel good."

"It's the drugs. They had no right sedating you," he replied firmly with some agitation in his tone. His eyes locked on her. "Answer my question."

She met his gaze only briefly while shifting uncomfortably. "They thought I was crazy," she replied almost timidly. "You will too."

"Let me decide for myself."

Jolynn studied him a moment in silence then frowned and drew a deep, shaken breath. The subject was very personal to her, and she'd never been treated kindly for admitting her deepest, darkest secret.

"I'm psychic," she finally blurted out, although that was the sugarcoated version of the truth.

"I see."

Slade set down his fork, leaned back in his seat, and gently tapped his fingers on the table. Although his expression didn't change, his eyes pierced through her.

"You're right," he boldly announced with little emotion. "I think you're crazy."

Jolynn groaned and sank back against the seat with her hand over her eyes. "Big surprise there," she muttered.

She couldn't believe even her eyes felt numb from the injection they'd given her. She'd never been so heavily sedated before. Jolynn made a conscious effort to retain her lucid thoughts, but it wasn't easy.

"But I'll hear you out," Slade then added as he shifted in his seat, his eyes never leaving hers. "So you had a vision that someone abducted your friend?"

Jolynn felt uneasy by the question. She straightened and managed to stare into his eyes, despite her inability to focus. "Not a vision," she attempted to explain, although she wasn't certain she was coherent enough to have this conversation. "More like a traumatic flash." She drew a deep breath and felt the all too familiar pang of fear when she'd attempt to explain the hell in which she lived. "Every time I touch someone, little pieces of their life flash in my mind. The more traumatic the event, the harder it hits. Sort of like being struck by lightning." She drew a shaken breath. "That's why I don't like being touched."

"Fair enough," he announced with little reaction. It was hard to tell if he believed her or was mocking her. "Did you also *see* who abducted Gillian?"

"Just a mask of darkness."

"Mask of darkness?" he suddenly asked, his brows knitting with confusion.

"Something so evil, it doesn't have a face," she informed him while fidgeting.

"Interesting," he replied with little reaction to the comment, indicating he didn't believe a word she was saying. "What else did you see?"

She didn't take her eyes off his as frustration built up inside her. "What's the point?" she muttered with a soft groan. "You don't believe me anyway."

He studied her a moment in silence then finally responded, "Maybe I do."

She glared at him, forcing her eyes to focus on the insufferable man. Her hostility was allowing her to cut through the sedation.

"I know when people are lying, *Agent Slade*," she hissed, driving her point home.

Slade sat back in the booth seat and stared at her, revealing a coy smile. "So make me believe you." He leaned forward and offered his hand.

Jolynn coiled back and stared at his hand as if it was a weapon. She met his gaze with a moderately concerned look. "You may want to reconsider," she suddenly remarked. "Do you have anything to hide?"

He slowly pulled his hand back, silently answering her question.

"I thought so," she stated with a slight hiss in her tone. "Place your badge on the table. It won't reveal all your deep dark secrets, and it'll be less traumatic for both of us."

Slade uncertainly reached into his jacket pocket, removed his badge, and set it on the table between them. Jolynn gently placed her hand on the leather casing and shut her eyes. Slade watched with great interest.

Jolynn's brows suddenly knitted with possible confusion as she touched the badge. "There are four men watching us," she informed him while keeping her eyes closed. "You've traveled to every small town within the county." Her eyes suddenly popped open, and she stared at him with bewilderment. "Looking for your pen pal?"

Slade stared a moment longer but showed little reaction. He then shifted in his seat. Although attempting to act casual, it was obvious he was suddenly uncomfortable.

"Very interesting."

She raised her hand from the leather badge holder as her expression turned arrogant. "The badge was made in Chicago by a man with a missing thumb," Jolynn proceeded to inform him. "You paid him two thousand dollars for it."

Slade quickly pulled the badge back while staring at her. His expression was hard to read.

She didn't take her accusing eyes from him. "An excellent forgery."

They exchanged stares only a moment. Her suspicions about him were finally founded. She knew he was a fraud. Slade casually returned the badge to his pocket.

"Very entertaining," Slade sneered hotly. "You should work in a circus sideshow."

She didn't appreciate him mocking her despite his knowing everything she said was true. Jolynn wasn't about to let the fraudulent federal agent get away with belittling her this time. She now had all the ammunition she needed to defeat him.

"Gillian's in a dark room with candles surrounding her," Jolynn informed him in a stern, serious tone. "She lying in a symbol painted in blood." Jolynn took his pen and drew on the paper napkin. "Around the symbol are fresh animal organs."

She finished the drawing on the napkin and pushed it before him. He stared at the symbol with little reaction then eyed her a long, silent moment. His fingers strummed the table then abruptly stopped.

"Jolynn, my dear, I just realized I need you more then you need me," Slade finally announced. "We can save your friend, but I'm going to need your help. I have to warn you, it won't be pleasant. Will you help me?"

She barely took time to consider the question before answering. "I'll do whatever it takes to get Gillian back alive," Jolynn informed him.

Slade drew a deep, tense breath. "I hope you mean that, because what I'm about to share with you is the sort of stuff nightmares are made of."

Chapter Seventeen

$\mathbf{J}$olynn left the diner with Slade and followed him to his newer model, black sedan. It was nearly sunup now. She still appeared unsteady and slightly foggy but finally felt more like her old self. A newer model black van jetted across the empty parking lot and practically skidded to a stop before them. Jolynn jumped with surprise as the side door vigorously slid open. Slade appeared unaffected by the appearance of the suspicious van, although Jolynn was moderately terrified. Slade offered her a tiny, reassuring smile and extended his hand to the open side door.

"After you."

Jolynn reluctantly climbed into the back of the van, joining the two men seated in the back. There were also two men in the front. The van contained a state-of-the-art computer system, looking like some high tech spy system. The high back, leather swivel chairs were bolted fast to the floor in front of the computer system. Obviously, they spared no expense for their technology. As the van door closed, Jolynn paid closer attention to the four men she had briefly seen in her vision while holding Slade's badge. Two of the men she recognized from Jerry's Tavern the night before Gillian disappeared.

One of the two men from the tavern was Carl, the one Gillian almost certainly would have pawned off on her. He was the shorter, moderately geeky looking guy in his late twenties with dark, curly hair and glasses. He seemed to be playing chauffeur to Slade's team. His co-pilot was Wilson, a much taller, physically fit African-American man in his mid-thirties. Wilson kept his black hair business neat the same as his wardrobe. Despite his size and build, his facial features lent a less intimidating and rather handsome appearance. Contrasting to Wilson's moderately lovable features, his counterpart, Rush, was the complete opposite.

Rush was intimidating from his solid build to his slightly balding head. The scar along the side of his right eye running two inches down his cheek didn't help ease his intimidating appearance. Jolynn found the scar almost as intimidating as his worn, leather jacket that possibly contained bullet holes. The last of the four-man boy band was the most complex of the group and the second man she'd seen at the tavern the other night. Baxter was built like a tank and twice as intimidating. His beady eyes tore through her. Perhaps he was still upset about being rejected by them the other night. Jolynn received unsettling looks from all four men, but their attention was soon focused on Slade. They obviously didn't approve of her presence, and she was certain they'd eventually express their feelings on the matter.

"What gives, Slade?" Carl practically demanded where he was sitting sideways behind the wheel.

Slade easily ignored the tone and offered a cheerful smile. "Welcome our newest member, Jolynn."

All four men appeared puzzled and exchanged unenthusiastic looks. Jolynn knew *unenthusiastic* was wishful thinking. She could tell they wanted her out of the van and out of their group. Rush looked *enthusiastic* to assist her out on his own. She doubted the man could crack a smile.

"Let's take a little drive, shall we?" Slade announced while maintaining his cheerful mood despite the attitude of the rest of his team.

Carl put the van into gear and drove away from the diner. Slade took a seat before the computer and pulled up several files. Horrible images of a murdered woman appeared on multiple screens. Jolynn stared at the images and could barely control her horrified gasp. The images were enough to turn her stomach.

"The Pen Pal kills his victims anywhere from one day to one week after abducting them. The pattern isn't much of a pattern so far. He kills in series of three then goes dormant for a few months. He usually sticks to small cities or towns in or around this county," Slade announced matter-of-fact, unaffected by the gruesome images. "Your friend will make number three if we don't stop him. Victim number two," he remarked and pulled up an image of Beth from a publicity photo taken of her, "is probably still alive, but she won't be for long. Time is running out for her."

Jolynn stared at the pictures and wished she could look away. The horrible images were going to stay with her a long time. She wasn't sure how they expected her to help some woman she'd never met on short notice, especially when she couldn't get Gillian out of her mind. And now the images were making concern for her friend even worse.

Slade casually leaned back in his chair and gave Jolynn his full attention. "He's your basic, garden-variety psychopath. All his victims are carefully chosen, sharing many of the same features. All are young and attractive with reddish colored hair. Interestingly enough, there is never any sign of sexual abuse." He rocked in his chair while briefly sinking into his own thoughts then jolted back to reality. "We've been tracking our friend a little over a year, but he's always been two steps ahead of us. In that time, he's killed ten women practically under our noses."

"Why don't you let the police handle this?" Jolynn finally asked.

"The police *are* handling this as well as the city homicide detective," Slade replied with little enthusiasm. "They aren't any closer to finding this guy than they were last year. They can't put all their effort into it, but we can." He drew a deep breath and leaned back in his chair. "A relative of the first victim, the wealthy eccentric type, contracted us to find the man responsible."

Jolynn studied the other men then looked back at Slade. "I'm not sure how I can help."

"I already have plans for you, my dear," Slade announced while grinning. "Just do as I say, and we may be able to find this guy before it's too late for Beth and Gillian." His look turned serious causing him to shift in his seat. "There's going to be a lot of unpleasantness involved. Consider yourself warned."

Jolynn held her breath then slowly nodded. She had to do whatever it took to save her friend. Especially after seeing the images on the screen, which were now burned into her mind. She certainly couldn't let that happen to Gillian.

"We have a studio apartment on the other side of town," Slade casually informed her. "We can take you there unless you think you'd have a better connection to Gillian in your own apartment."

Her mind was already reeling with the information Slade had given. It took a moment for his comment to sink in.

"It helps to be in their world," Jolynn replied, feeling her own body twitch with insecurity. "She has certain items in her room that might keep me close to her."

Slade nodded then looked to the driver. "Carl, take us back to the diner for my car." He glanced at the other men. "I'd like to take Jolynn to the town theater later tomorrow morning." He cast a look at Jolynn. "That's where the second girl was abducted." Slade returned his attention to his men. "We'll meet with you in the afternoon at the abandoned warehouse. I'll take Jolynn back to her apartment and let her get a few hours' sleep before we put her to work."

Jolynn eyed him, tensing slightly from his comment, but she didn't protest. For Gillian's sake, she just hoped he knew what he was doing.

Chapter Eighteen

Jolynn entered her apartment with some apprehension. It seemed almost foreign knowing Gillian was there when she left and was now God knows where. Everything was as she had left it, a grim reminder that a normal day could suddenly change in the blink of an eye. Slade followed her into the apartment, shutting and locking the door behind him. He looked around as if expecting to find something pertinent to Gillian's abduction. Jolynn rubbed her shoulders insecurely, feeling uneasy with some man she barely knew joining her in her home. Particularly *that* man.

"It's really not necessary for you to stay here," she informed him. "If you're right about Gillian's kidnapper, he's certainly not coming back here."

"There's a lot we don't know about this guy," Slade remarked. "I'd rather not take any chances. Do you have a current photo of Gillian?"

Jolynn nodded, allowing her arms to fall to her side. She approached the entertainment cabinet and removed a framed picture of her and Gillian taken on the deck of a boat during one of their day trips. As she turned, Slade approached, meeting her halfway and briefly studied the photo before removing it from the frame. He placed it in his inner jacket pocket for safekeeping and again looked around before meeting her gaze.

"Is there anything you need to help make a connection?" he asked.

"It doesn't always work that way," Jolynn replied. "Sometimes an object will work; other times visions just come on their own. I never know what will trigger a vision." She considered her own comment. She'd never forced herself to make a connection before, so she wasn't even sure how to get started. Too often, she spent time avoiding things that would trigger a psychic reaction. "I'll sleep in Gillian's room tonight. Being immersed in her world may help." She then hesitated and shifted uncomfortably. "You, uh, can sleep in my room, if you'd like."

"Only if you're okay with that."

She inhaled deeply then sighed while drifting out slightly. "I have far bigger concerns right now."

Slade nodded in response then gave her a serious look. "If anything comes to you, no matter how unimportant it seems, wake me immediately."

Jolynn nodded and managed a tiny smile. As she headed for Gillian's room, she couldn't help think how different Slade was compared with earlier that morning at the hospital records department. Maybe he wasn't as big of a prick as she'd originally thought. At the very least, he was dedicated to helping her find Gillian. For that, she was grateful.

†

Gillian sat bound and gagged in the center of the dingy candlelit room of what appeared to be an old farmhouse. The bland walls and floor were old plank wood with a heavy layer of dust and dirt covering them. The unusually large, old window was boarded from the outside making it impossible to see her location. Gillian had been fighting the duct tape that bound her wrists since she regained consciousness. Her continuing effort to free herself left her wrists chafed and bloodied from the friction of the tape. She could hear strange noises from somewhere within the old building. She stopped struggling long enough to listen to the sounds and perhaps get a fix on her location. She heard a train in the distance. The sound of the train wasn't enough to tell her where she was, but sounds of life outside her prison almost comforted her. It meant help wasn't that far away, if she could only reach it.

Stiff muscles and exhaustion had just about gotten the best of her when she managed to free her right hand. She let out a relieved gasp and pulled the tape from her mouth. Gillian almost sobbed at the small taste of freedom, but she was far from there just yet. She fumbled with the tape around her ankles and finally managed to unbind her feet. She sprang to her feet and nearly fell back down from her lengthy, awkward positon on the hard floor. She looked around the room, breathing heavily with added anxiety, and assessed her situation.

There was blood along the walls, which resembled crude writing in some unknown language, adding to her fears. It was time to leave. She approached the door and gently turned the knob, quickly discovering it was locked. It wouldn't be her luck that the door was unlocked. She didn't dare struggle with it in case her abductor was nearby. He couldn't know she was free. Gillian hurried to the boarded window and attempted open it, but the window was painted shut possibly decades ago. With each attempt, she sobbed hysterically as frustration got the better of her. She looked back at the door and once again approached it. Gillian pulled on the door with a little more vigor while trying to keep from making too much noise.

Since the door opened inward, casting her body against it would do little good. She ran trembling fingers through her hair, hesitated while considering something, and then fumbled within her pockets. All were emptied. A thought then occurred to her. She removed her credit card from her cleavage and almost had to laugh at the irony. She inserted the card between the door and the jam. The door was possibly old enough for the trick to work. It took several minutes, but the door eventually popped open. Gillian never felt so relieved in her life. She cast the card aside and slowly opened the door, attempting to keep the creaking of the old hinges to a minimum.

She peered into the hallway, giving her a better sense of where she was being held. She was in an old farmhouse of some sort. Gillian slowly crept along the second floor hallway of the dilapidated, old house and looked around cautiously. The light poking in from the dirty, mostly boarded hall window was just bright enough to allow her to see where she was going. It seemed to be dawn and the light possibly came from a streetlamp. She quietly hurried along the hall toward the frightening looking stairs. The railing was broken in spots and there were missing boards on the old stairs. She could hear the hall floorboards creaking beneath her with each step as it was. The stairs would be tricky if she wanted to make as little noise as possible. She had to assume her abductor was in the house, and that he would hear her making the great escape. There was little choice though.

Gillian made her way as quickly and quietly as possible down the stairs that still creaked loudly with each step. Once she realized she was unable to take the steps without any sound, she picked up the pace as she neared the bottom. Once she hit the last step, she ran for the front door. She swore she saw a shadow out of the corner of her eye within one of the darkened rooms, but she wasn't about to stop and check it out. Gillian pulled on the door, but it wouldn't open. She yanked harder, determined to break it if she had to. She practically felt the shadow looming over her now. Gillian gasped and spun around, facing her abductor. Her look shattered at his presence, causing her to scream.

Chapter Nineteen

Jolynn was nestled beneath the thick comforter on Gillian's bed, sleeping peacefully while clinging to one of her friend's favorite stuffed animals. Her dreams were distorted and appeared to make little sense. She saw Gillian curled in the corner of a dingy, empty room resembling something from a haunted house. Her friend was no longer tied, but she shivered and sobbed softly. The images of writing in blood on the walls surrounded her. Her dream quickly morphed to an old farmhouse porch. Jolynn stood on the porch and looked around the vast farmland in the middle of nowhere. She had no idea where she was, but she was alone. She turned toward the old, rustic door and stood before a huge grim reaper in a flowing black cloak with only darkness beyond his hood. He slashed at her with his sling blade.

Jolynn screamed and ran from the porch. Instead of running across the overgrown farmland, which was the direction she headed, she discovered she was now inside the old farmhouse. There were candles burning everywhere and blood was painted on the walls and floor. She stopped in the hallway and quickly turned, wanting to leave, when she ran into a faceless, familiar man. She didn't know who he was, but she threw her arms around him, clinging to him. As he held her against him, she felt her entire body relax. For a moment, she was at peace. When she opened her eyes, she saw the faceless man prevent a shadowy figure of a monster from attacking her. Jolynn watched in horror as the shadow monster tore him apart. She screamed at the gruesome sight then looked at the shadow monster as it morphed into a black creature covered in her hero's blood. She screamed while staring at the blood-covered beast about to attack her.

There was a brilliant flash taking her from the violent dream. She now stood helplessly in an elegant study made of rich dark wood and witnessed Slade kneeling over a young woman's bloodied butchered body. His hands were covered in the woman's blood. Jolynn suddenly screamed, flew up in Gillian's bed, and slammed her back against the headboard. Slade sat on the bed facing her with a startled look on his face. She looked around Gillian's room with some disorientation then stared at Slade before her.

"You were screaming in your sleep," he announced in a soft nervous tone, appearing almost as terrified as she was.

Jolynn gasped several times and allowed her head to fall into her hands. "I told you not to touch me," she proclaimed softly then looked at him. "What were you trying to do? Kill me?"

"Sounded like you were already being killed," he replied while fumbling with his hands, uncertain what to do with them. "What did you dream? Anything that will help?"

She took several deep breaths while attempting to control her pounding heart before responding. "I saw Gillian in an empty room with more writing in blood on the walls," she informed him then insecurely rubbed her chilled arms. "I don't think he's hurt her yet. She's just scared. Nothing to indicate where she is, although we may be looking for a farmhouse."

"Maybe the warehouse will give you more information," Slade announced then eyed her suspiciously and hesitated. "Was there anything else?"

Jolynn sighed and glanced at him with a tired, harsh expression. "No, just my usual brush with death dreams."

"You dream you die?"

"No, but since I was about thirteen, I've dreamt of this man who saves me from a monster and dies tragically at its hands," she gently informed him. "I believe he's supposed to be my one true love. Someone I haven't met yet."

"But he dies," Slade interjected with an odd look. "Where's the fun it that?"

"We all have our destinies, Mr. Slade," she informed him. "We can't change them. They're predetermined."

Slade studied her a moment then offered a mocking smile. "That's what you choose to believe," he teased. "And hiding in that basement of yours pretty much seals your fate. The rest of us make it up as we go."

"If I could keep others from entering my head, I'm sure I'd be a little more outgoing," she retorted. "But since I have little say in the matter, it's best to avoid all physical contact, especially from those with tainted pasts."

"I guess that includes me."

Jolynn stared at him without comment. He met her gaze and attempted a warm smile.

"Seriously, I'm not all that bad."

Jolynn continued to stare then returned the smile. "I'm sure you're not." There was a brief silence between them. She raised her curious brow. "Who was she?"

Slade's expression dropped with concern. "Who?"

"You touched me right before I woke," she informed him. "I saw you kneeling over a dead woman with blood on your hands. Who was she?"

Slade suddenly tensed and shifted on the bed. "You'd better get a few more hours' sleep. We have a long day ahead of us."

He quickly stood and left the room.

✝

𝐽erry's Tavern was mostly dead as usual for early afternoon on a Saturday. The evening would be packed with locals celebrating the happiest day of the weekend. Loni sat at the bar, slumped over her drink. She didn't have the look of a girl happy to celebrate the weekend. For the theater company, it was a time or mourning. Not knowing what happened to Beth had everyone at the theater upset as well. There was hope they'd find their cast mate alive and well, but the condition of their director suggested it was little more than wishful thinking. With so few patrons, Jerry joined Loni and leaned on the bar from his side.

"Any word on Beth?" he asked with a sympathetic look.

Loni groaned softly and shook her head. "No, nothing so far."

"Sheriff Gruber has been pretty tight-lipped since he's been working with the city homicide detective," Jerry announced while remaining slumped on the bar. "It'd be nice to know something. I mean, first Wendy and now Beth's been kidnapped."

Loni gave him a stunned look. "So it's true," she nearly gasped. "The woman they found in the warehouse was Wendy?"

"Oh, I thought you knew," he said while straightening. "Just because Wendy was murdered, that doesn't mean it's the same creep who took Beth. I'm confident they'll find her alive."

"I appreciate your optimism," Loni replied gently. "Do they have any leads at all about who killed Wendy?"

"They'd like to question a few of the male patrons she'd gotten friendly with," Jerry informed her. "It's just such a long list; they're having a tough time finding all of them."

"Well, Wendy was a friendly girl," Loni announced delicately.

"Personally, I think they should be looking at the long line of jilted women," Jerry informed her. "I remember this one woman went out of her mind. Caught her boyfriend getting it on with Wendy in the women's bathroom. They got into one hell of a cat fight in the back."

"Really? What happened?"

"Yelling, screaming, profanity, and hair pulling," he replied with a casual shrug. "The woman was pissed though. She ended up leaving with the other man at her table. I'm guessing she got her revenge on her boyfriend with that one."

Loni stared at Jerry then sank into thought. She appeared curious. "The guy getting it on with Wendy," she announced. "Was he that cute but nerdy looking guy?"

"I'll go with nerdy," Jerry remarked. "I don't know that I'd consider him cute. Seen him in here a few times with different women."

"Yeah," Loni remarked and became distant. "I think I remember that incident." She quickly stood and grabbed her purse. "I, uh, have to get to the theater. They police are allowing us to rehearse this afternoon, and I don't want to be late."

Loni hurried away from the bar and headed outside. Once she left the tavern, she removed her cell phone from her purse and dialed a single number. The phone was almost immediately picked up.

"Deputy Hunt," came the male voice.

"Hey, Hunt," she announced while nervously looking around. "It's Loni."

"Loni," he replied with a hint of enthusiasm then attempted to sound sympathetic. "No news on Beth yet."

"No, that's not why I'm calling," she informed him and paced the tavern porch. "Jerry just reminded me of an incident involving Wendy a few weeks ago. She got into a fight with a woman over a man."

"Yeah, we still haven't narrowed down the man or woman involved in that incident," he replied.

"Well, it's not just that," Loni reported. "I know it's going to sound like gossip, but I think we need to discuss other incidents prior to that. I don't know if it means anything, but it might be important. Can you meet me at the theater in an hour? I have rehearsal, and I can't be late."

"Uh, sure."

"We can talk afterwards," she informed him. "I'd feel better if you walked me home tonight anyway."

"Sure," he replied. "I'm just finishing up here at the morgue. I'll be there in an hour."

"Great," she announced with a relieved sigh. "I'll see you then."

She disconnected the call while staring across the nearly empty tavern parking lot and shivered slightly.

Chapter Twenty

The Linville Theater remained closed since the murder and abduction, giving the surrounding area an eerie presence in the early afternoon. The shopping district where the theater was located was particularly quiet but would be alive with activity later in the evening. Loni walked through the alley from the back parking lot and headed toward the side, alleyway entrance. She seemed a little more tense than usual and looked around every few feet. She'd inadvertently arrived nearly an hour early for their rehearsal, which didn't help her anxiety any.

The alley was quiet and contained very little opportunity for someone to hide, so her anxiety was unfounded. Still, she kept watch over her shoulder. She approached the bland, metal door to the theater and inserted her key into the old-fashioned lock. When she turned the key, she didn't hear the typical click as it unlocked, which meant someone had already unlocked the door for their arrival. She again glanced over her shoulder before hurrying into the theater. Loni walked along the cluttered backstage region, feeling the need to scan the area several times. Someone was obviously within the theater somewhere, but it didn't ease her nervous condition. She considered calling out but kept quiet instead. Running into the creepy janitor wasn't a comforting thought.

She left the backstage area and entered the eerily silent side hallway, which lead past several dressing rooms reserved for the stars of the show. She paused before Beth's dressing room, briefly stared at the flimsy nameplate, and insecurely rubbed her chilled shoulders for some unknown reason. The nameplates, although a symbol of status upon a dressing room door, were grimly two-fold. They were cheap and easily removed, allowing a star to be here today and gone just as easily tomorrow. Loni drew a deep breath then entered Beth's dressing room. She had been sharing the coveted room with her friend, so she had many of her belongings in regards to the play still within Beth's dressing room.

She turned on the light, which brightened the room considerably. The room appeared untouched, although the police had searched the dressing room after Beth's disappearance. Either they did a lousy search, or they were careful not to disturb much. Loni turned toward the costume rack then hesitated and looked back at the dressing table with its brilliant lights surrounding the large mirror. Several photos were stuck into the side of the mirror. Loni approached the dressing table and studied the photos. There were plenty of her with Beth, a tribute to their close friendship. She saw one in particular that caught her attention.

Loni removed the photo from the mirror. The picture of the two was a selfie taken at Jerry's tavern. Loni strained to look in the background behind them. She could make out three people at the table behind them. Her eyes suddenly lit up. Despite the horrible lighting and blurred images, she realized it was a picture of the man Jerry had mentioned in connection with Wendy. The woman in the picture with him was also a redhead. The police were having a difficult time figuring out who had been involved in the bathroom fling and ensuing fight. If she could find a better picture from that evening, it could help the police locate the man and woman for questioning. Loni routed through Beth's dressing table drawers and attempted to find more pictures. The drawers were cluttered with everything from make-up to props. Loni finally found a stack of photos. She shuffled through them, stopped on one in particular, and dropped the rest. She stared at the photo as her eyes lit up.

"This is it," she softly proclaimed.

Loni looked around the dressing room as if expecting someone to be standing behind her. When it was obvious no one was there, she only gave it a moment's thought before stuffing the photo down the front of her shirt. She would need to find Deputy Hunt the moment he arrived at the theater. Helping with the investigation was more important than discussing who would be the new director and what would become of their upcoming production. None of that seemed important at the moment. All that mattered was finding Beth *alive.*

Loni headed for the open dressing room door. The theater was so quiet, it almost didn't seem possible that anyone else was there, but someone must have been or the door wouldn't have been left unlocked. The janitor must have unlocked it in anticipation of the others arriving for the rehearsal. Loni then hesitated and thought of something less comforting. Or had the janitor unlocked the door for his favorite homeless man? Was it possible Derek was lurking about the theater? She drew a deep, nervous breath and attempted to brush the thought from her mind. She headed along the corridor and approached the backstage door. As she passed through the doorway, the lights suddenly went out throughout the entire theater. Loni suddenly froze. Although it wouldn't be the first time the lights spontaneously went out, the thought was slightly more chilling at the moment.

Just as she was about to cross the backstage area, she saw the janitor enter through another side door with his flashlight. Loni suddenly tensed and darted behind the wardrobe rack to avoid being seen by the man. It was childish to hide from the man, especially when there was nothing to indicate he had anything to do with what happened to Beth or Tyler. Despite that, she remained hidden and quiet behind the wardrobe rack. The janitor vanished into the chaos of the cluttered backstage area, his light no longer visible. He was undoubtedly heading in the direction of the basement and the fuse box to restore the lights. She sighed with relief and placed a trembling hand to her forehead. She finally stepped out from behind the wardrobe rack and nearly collided with a large, nearby prop. She reached out to feel the prop, in order to decipher her location. Loni felt something thin and metal.

She ran her hand along the metal object, feeling a sharp tip. She was about to pull her hand back when the sharp object pierced her hand, running straight through her palm. She screamed at the agonizing pain, uncertain what she'd managed to run into, and at the same time trying to figure out where the nearest exit was, since she knew she was bleeding. The object was pulled from her hand, causing nearly the same amount of pain but now adding the realization that she hadn't run into something sharp, but rather something sharp had been thrust into her. Loni cried out while leaping backward a step, striking the wardrobe rack. She lost her balance and fell into the rack filled with costumes, which kept her from falling through and to the floor. She attempted to maintain her balance while catching her first glimpse of the predator before her. In the darkness, all she could see was the dark outline of a man with scraggly hair and jagged facial features. Although she could barely see him, she was certain he was no one she'd ever encountered before.

Loni managed to scream but only briefly as the outline of a dagger appeared in what little light remained by the glow of the emergency exit sign. She watched in horror as the dagger was thrust downward, embedding deep into her neck. The pain was intense, but she was now unable to scream as blood filled her throat. The scream became a rush of blood flowing from her mouth. She clutched the clothing on the wardrobe rack practically surrounding her now. She struggled to keep her balance, but her head quickly became light. What little light remained in the room turned to darkness as she sank into the hanging costumes. The killer plunged the dagger into her chest for added measure. He was about to strike again when a door was heard opening from somewhere in the auditorium. The killer pulled the costumes together, hiding the fallen starlet now on the floor beneath the rack.

Chapter Twenty-one

Slade and Jolynn stood toward the back of the auditorium near the open doors. Light shining into the lobby from the outside world was the only thing brightening the auditorium. Jolynn looked around and uncertainly rubbed her chilled arms.

"Uh, it's a little dark in there," she announced, unwilling to enter any further.

"There must be lights somewhere," Slade replied while removing a small flashlight from his pocket.

As his tiny light scanned the nearby walls, several houselights suddenly came on, partially brightening the once dark auditorium. Jolynn and Slade exchanged looks.

Slade shrugged. "I guess they saw us arrive," he announced without care. "Would you like me to show you around?"

She slowly shook her head. "No," Jolynn gently replied and again rubbed her chilled arms while inhaling deeply. "I think I'd like a little space. Solitude is best."

He offered a tiny smile and nodded. She slowly walked down the aisle toward the stage and looked around. There were several images invading her senses, but she was positive not all of them involved what happened the other night. What was it about theaters that reminded her of a haunted place? As Jolynn approached the stage, she instinctively paused just a few feet from it and looked down at the tacky carpet beneath her feet. Her attention was drawn to the bloodstains left behind from the attack. Someone made an attempt to clean the carpet but was unsuccessful. She drew a shaken breath then slowly circled the bloodstain without taking her eyes off it. Slade watched her from a distant, taking in her entire process without comment. Jolynn could hear Beth's screams from that horrible night. The sound of the knife piercing Tyler's body was almost too chilling to withstand. The images from that night began flashing in her mind as she relived Tyler's last moments and Beth's turmoil.

"Hey, what are you people doing here?" a voice suddenly demanded, startling Jolynn. "The theater's closed!"

The attack vanished from Jolynn's subconscious as she focused on the man approaching from the side stage door. As the janitor approached Jolynn, Slade walked down the aisle to greet him while flashing his badge.

"It's okay," Slade informed him. "I'm with the FBI. We're investigating the attack and abduction that took place here the other night."

The janitor eyed Slade suspiciously then looked at Jolynn, who hadn't moved from Tyler's death scene. The janitor seemed to relax slightly then gave a slight nod at the bloodstains on the floor near Jolynn's feet.

"That's where Tyler got it," the janitor remarked with a defeated sigh. He eyed Slade and cocked his head slightly to the side. "Are they checking into her boyfriend? They'd broken up the week before. A bit of a hothead, that one. They found him here along with another fellow standing over Tyler's body."

"I believe the police questioned both men excessively," Slade informed him. "They haven't found enough evidence to detain either. Do you spend a lot of time around the theater?"

"Certainly do. I have a room in the attic," the janitor informed him while giving a slight nod toward the ceiling. "Though I didn't see anything that night. I didn't know anything had happened until I heard the fire alarm sound."

"Do you remember seeing anyone who didn't belong hanging around the theater that night?" Slade questioned.

The janitor shook his head without hesitation. "No, just Derek."

"Derek?"

"Just some homeless man," the janitor replied. "Been hanging around a few months. I give him leftovers and sometimes let him sleep in the back when the weather's bad."

There was an awkward silence. Slade's mind was obviously reeling with the new information.

"Do you know where he is?" Slade asked in an unusually calm tone, although his eyes told a different story.

"No, I couldn't say," the janitor replied then waved him off. "He's harmless. Docile sort of fella." The janitor insecurely placed his hands in his pockets and seemed to shift from foot-to-foot. "Haven't seen him around since the killing," he offered a little too quickly. "Police coming and going tends to frighten the homeless people away."

"I'll bet," Slade muttered while obviously coming to his own conclusion. He turned to Jolynn. "I need to have a look around outside. Wait here. See if you can gain any insight but don't wonder off too far."

Jolynn nodded and watched Slade return up the aisle with a mission in mind.

The janitor appeared suspicious and eyed Jolynn. "He doesn't suspect Derek, does he?"

"Certainly looks that way."

The janitor waved her off with some disgust and possible hostility. "Barking up the wrong tree, if you ask me," he muttered. "I'll be in the back if you need me."

Jolynn watched the man walk onto stage in a little more of a hurry then disappear behind the curtain. It was possible the janitor was a little overly protective of Derek, the homeless man. For the first time, she was left alone in the auditorium. Jolynn nervously rubbed her chilled arms and looked around. It didn't take long for her senses to pick up on the fresh events from that deadly night. She heard Beth's terrified screams and the horrifying images once again flashed in her mind.

✝

Slade walked through the alley alongside the theater. Alleys in smaller cities weren't nearly as menacing as those in bigger cities were. There were some garbage cans and recycling bins lined along the building exteriors but very little misplaced trash. He paused just outside the theater's side door, which some of the theater performers used as a more direct route to the back parking lot. Slade pulled on the door but naturally, it was locked. He continued through the alley toward the back parking lot access. Someone was heard up ahead. Slade approached more cautiously but quickened his pace. He arrived in the parking lot, but there wasn't anyone there.

Chapter Twenty-two

Voices from backstage interrupted Jolynn's visions, causing her to focus on the present rather than the past. Jolynn appeared curious while staring at the stage then approached the steps. She slowly walked up the few steps to the stage and heard the voices a little clearer than before.

"You'd better get out of here before you're seen," a man's voice spoke.

She heard what sounded like more than one person moving around behind the curtain backstage. Jolynn silently stepped behind the curtain and looked around the moderately cluttered area. There was no one there. Although she was surprised she hadn't found anyone, she also knew there were several escape routes and even more hiding places if someone wanted to avoid being seen. She walked along the area backstage then suddenly stopped as a startling image shot through her mind. Within her vision, she saw the janitor clutching his bleeding throat. The vision was enough to frighten her. Jolynn gasped and quickly turned, colliding with Dawson. Both jumped with surprise. In the brief moment she connected with Dawson, she saw a flash of him with Beth in a rather compromising position. Jolynn couldn't erase the erotic image from her mind, forcing her to stare at the handsome Columbian man standing before her.

"Who are you?" Dawson demanded in a gruff voice, although his tone conveyed concern more than hostility. "What are you doing here?"

"Uh, I'm here with Agent Slade of the FBI," she fumbled with her response. "He's investigating the abduction of the young actress from the other night." She nervously looked around, not wanting to be alone with the unfamiliar man. Something about him made her uneasy. "I seem to have lost the janitor."

"He's probably in the back somewhere as usual." Dawson seemed unusually tense and avoided looking her in the eyes. "Are they any closer to finding Beth?" he asked in a slightly gruff tone, indicating his annoyance with either their presence or the entire situation. "Anything I can do to help?"

"I think we should find Agent Slade," Jolynn informed him, feeling her own nerves twitch after her frightening premonition. "He went outside to have a look around. Something about a suspicious homeless guy."

"They think that guy killed Tyler and abducted Beth?" His eyes narrowed and the veins in his temples bulged. "I know where he hides," he declared in his thick accent.

Without awaiting a response, Dawson hurried across the backstage area toward the first exit door. Jolynn attempted to follow him, hurrying after him past the large wardrobe rack.

"We should wait for Agent Slade," she called after him, not liking the vibes she was getting.

She didn't even notice the large pool of blood rapidly collecting on the floor beneath the wardrobe rack. Jolynn reached Dawson by the back exit and cut him off before he could open the door. She held up a trembling hand, although she didn't dare touch him.

"I *really* think we should wait for Agent Slade," Jolynn insisted.

He gave her an odd once over, obviously noting her frightened demeanor and seemed baffled by it. "What sort of FBI agent are you?"

"I'm not an agent," she blurted out then hesitated. She hated the words that next came from her mouth. "I'm, uh, the resident psychic."

Dawson's disgust was evident as he rolled his eyes, mocking her 'profession'. "Maybe you'd better wait here."

He brushed her aside and hurried through the back door. Although thankful he hadn't actually touched her, Jolynn felt her tension rising. It was almost as if she could feel death all around her and not in the past tense sort of way. She insecurely rubbed her shoulders while looking around with concern. She saw a shadow near the wardrobe rack. She didn't know who it was, but her fear was real. She wanted to bolt after Dawson, but an image flashed through her mind with tremendous force, causing her to clutch her temples. She saw the bloody, jagged dagger as Beth's screams echoed through her mind. Jolynn struggled to make sense of her visions and stop the physical pain they were causing her. She then heard Slade from somewhere within the auditorium.

"Jolynn," Slade called out. "Where are you?"

Jolynn released her temples and took a quick step closer to the stage curtain near the wardrobe rack. She slipped, catching her balance, and instinctively looked down. She discovered she was standing within a pool of blood spilling out from beneath the wardrobe rack. Horror crossed her face. She was about to scream when an image of the bloody dagger striking downward flashed violently within her mind, although she couldn't see who was on the receiving end. Jolynn suddenly leaped away from the wardrobe rack as if dodging the imaginary dagger. The wardrobe rack vibrated slightly, filling her with fear.

"Slade," she screamed hysterically while bolting for the stage curtain.

She reached for the end of the curtain and nearly collided with Slade, who had been attempting to reach her. His concern was genuine as he reached out to touch her but caught himself and resisted the action.

"What's wrong?" he demanded. "What happened?"

Jolynn pointed to the nearby wardrobe rack and the large pool of blood collecting beneath it.

She practically shouted in a whisper, "He's there!"

Slade removed his gun, which was affixed with a silencer, from his shoulder holster and quickly but cautiously approached the wardrobe rack. He parted the costumes with his left hand and aimed his gun at the dead woman. As he stared at the dead actress, he cringed slightly. He lowered his gun and looked back at Jolynn.

"It's one of the actresses from the theater company," he informed her with defeat. "She's been murdered."

"I'm telling you, he's here," she insisted while attempting to control her hysteria.

Slade read her eyes then continued his search with his gun leading the way. He cautiously approached the second stage door just beyond the wardrobe rack.

Jolynn wrenched her fingers together as her heart pounded. "Be careful."

Before he could grasp the knob, the door suddenly opened. Slade leaped into the doorway and pulled Dawson into the backstage area, slamming his back against the wall. Dawson cried out at the gun aimed at his face.

Slade slowly relaxed his grip on Dawson's shirt and frowned. "Who the hell are you?" he demanded while keeping his gun trained on the man.

"Dawson Hayes," he cried out in a slightly shrill voice while staring at the gun still aimed at him. "I'm just an actor, I swear! I work here at the theater. I can show you my ID!"

"That's Beth's ex-boyfriend," Jolynn reluctantly informed Slade.

"Believe her," Dawson nervously announced while pointing. "She's psychic."

Slade released the frightened man and finally lowered his gun. "Yes, I remember," he announced. "You were gone before I arrived on the scene."

Dawson looked at the dead woman surrounded by blood on the floor beneath the wardrobe rack. "Oh, my God! Loni," he cried out with horror then looked at Slade. "Did you kill her?"

Slade glared his annoyance at the man. "No, I didn't kill her," he scoffed. "I'd never even met her."

Jolynn eyed Slade suspiciously. "Then how did you know she was an actress?"

Slade gave her a sideways glare but didn't respond. The janitor entered the area and looked at the men.

"What's going on back here?" the janitor demanded. He then saw the dead actress on the floor beneath the wardrobe. Shock filled his eyes before he tore them away from the sight. "Loni," he gasped with horror.

The lights backstage suddenly went out. Jolynn let out a startled cry. The area remained dimly lit from the lights still on within the auditorium showing beneath the heavy curtains. There seemed to be shadows moving from everywhere. A large shadow then emerged from a dark corner, light glistening off the dagger blade. Jolynn saw the outline of the killer along with her vision of the dagger and screamed in response, alerting the three men. The sounds of thumping feet were heard running across the wooden backstage floor. All three men were plowed down by the shadowy figure. Slade's gun discharged from the hard hit, although with the silencer, the shot was barely heard. There were several groans and someone cried out.

Jolynn held back her scream and attempted to see what was happening within the darkness. She looked around, wondering where the nearest light switch was located. There was a loud scuffle from the floor then the sound of something crashing. The backstage hallway door was thrown open, momentarily flooding light into the otherwise dark backstage area. Jolynn saw the brief outline of a man running into the hallway. She frantically felt the wall near her and found the light switch.

The lights came on, brightening the entire area backstage. Slade, the janitor, and Dawson remained sprawled on the floor beneath several stage props. Jolynn ran for all three men. As she approached, Slade tossed some stage props off him and held his bleeding right, upper arm. He turned toward Dawson, who was less than a foot away from him. He also clutched his bleeding upper arm while glaring at Slade.

"You bastard," he cried out while looking at the bleeding scratch on his left arm beneath his hand then glared back at Slade. "You shot me!"

"It's just a scratch," Slade snarled with little emotion while clinging to his own injury. "Don't be such a drama queen."

As Dawson went into a rant, Jolynn and Slade ignored him and looked at the janitor as he attempted to stand. The look on his face resembled terror. The janitor stumbled slightly, gasped loudly, and immediately clutched his neck as blood poured from the razor thin cut. He looked at Jolynn and attempted to speak but he only gurgled up blood. Slade sprang into action, tossing Jolynn his cell phone as he leaped to the janitor's side. He immediately applied pressure to the bleeding wound. Dawson stared at the dying janitor with horror and appeared unable to move. Within the struggle in the dark, it very easily could have been any one of them bleeding to death.

Chapter Twenty-three

Linville Hospital had very little activity despite being late afternoon. The hospital was seldom busy and most of the patients were locals with simple ailments seeing the various doctors renting office space. Jolynn stood alongside the exam table within the private examination room and watched the doctor stitch the slice on Slade's right, upper arm. She clung to her chilled arms and grimaced at the suture process, although she'd occasionally steal peeks at Slade's bare chest and broad shoulders. Moments like these were when she missed human contact. Unmistakably handsome, she hadn't dreamed he'd look so good without a shirt.

Her minor fantasy was again ruined by the doctor tugging on another stitch, as he closed up the fleshy, gaping wound. Slade didn't care to watch while the doctor stitched him, but he occasionally glanced at Jolynn and noted the faces she'd make throughout the process. For a guy using a federal agent as his cover, he seemed almost squeamish by her slightly sickened expression. He started breathing again once the doctor began bandaging his arm. Sheriff Gruber entered the exam room, eyed Slade, and shook his head.

"That's two more chilling in the morgue thanks to you," the sheriff boldly announced. "Our town didn't have a murder rate until you showed up, Agent Slade."

"No, Sheriff," Slade announced with a sigh. "I showed up because you had a murder rate. There's a difference." He put on a tough act in front of the sheriff, but Jolynn knew Slade was feeling a bit nauseous from his ordeal. "Were you able to locate the homeless guy? What's his name? Derek?"

"No, not yet," Sheriff Gruber replied with a sigh, "but we'll find him. He always shows up eventually, especially around dinnertime. I have eyes and ears at all his favorite dinner stops. Someone will report him by tonight." He shook his head. "I think you're barking up the wrong tree, Agent Slade. Derek isn't a killer. Slightly unbalanced and a bit reclusive, but certainly not a killer. I questioned him after Tyler was killed at the theater. Tyler and the janitor were some of his best allies. They'd even let him sleep in the theater on cold nights. He wouldn't kill either of them, and he'd certainly have no reason to abduct Beth."

"I'd like to question him anyway," Slade informed him.

"I'll pick him up and arrange a face-to-face meeting, but I doubt he'll say much in front of you," Sheriff Gruber replied. "He doesn't know you, which means he won't trust you." The sheriff inhaled a deep breath. "I'm actually more interested in the alleged boyfriend. The one who showed up late to meet Beth that night. He's not originally from around here."

"I read your report from that interview, and he didn't fit the profile," Slade informed him. "Besides, he has alibies for the other murders earlier in the year."

"Isn't it possible those murders are unrelated," Sheriff Gruber suggested while raising a cocky brow. "You don't know that Beth's disappearance and Tyler's murder are in anyway connected to your serial killer. I mean, has your killer ever come back to a crime scene and kill potential witnesses?"

"No, not in the year I've been hunting him, but I'm still convinced they're connected," Slade replied. "If you want to question the suspects with a different assumption, feel free to go your own direction with your investigation. We're both working toward the same goal of stopping a killer."

"I'm glad you feel that way," Gruber announced and rested his thumbs within his holster. "I think the theater killings have more to do with Beth than some serial killer. The detective on the case seems to agree with me too."

"Fine, Sheriff," Slade replied while gingerly slipping into his bloodied shirt. "You conduct your investigation, and I'll conduct mine."

Sheriff Gruber finally looked at Jolynn. "Can I assume your friend returned home safe and sound?"

"No, Sheriff," she remarked lowly with irritation in her tone. She couldn't hide her detest for Sheriff Gruber. "I'm counting on

Agent Slade to find her though." She glanced at Slade. "I'll be in the waiting room."

Jolynn walked past Sheriff Gruber without looking at him. Gruber shook his head and watched her leave.

"Something's not right with that girl," the sheriff remarked.

"Actually, Sheriff, if you'd take the time to listen to her, you'd learn to appreciate how useful she can really be," Slade announced as he jumped off the exam table. "Happy hunting, Sheriff."

†

Slade and Jolynn left the hospital through the outpatient exit and approached Slade's black car parked in the nearly empty parking lot. Slade painfully flexed his wrapped right arm. His torn, bloody shirt was a constant reminder of the incident at the theater just a few hours earlier. Jolynn couldn't help but feel sorry for Slade despite his tough act. She knew the risk he took, and the janitor's fate could easily have been his own. It seemed unlikely the killer was singling out the janitor. He'd have little reason. Although, Dawson could have just as easily been the intended target. At the risk of siding with Sheriff Gruber, Jolynn knew the killer's reason for returning to the theater seemed sketchy at best. If the janitor was the intended target all along, then that would mean the homeless man had to be the Pen Pal. The janitor was the only one who'd easily identify him and perhaps even knew more than he had admitted.

"Are you sure you're okay?" she asked sympathetically while cringing at his bloodied torn shirt. She was still amazed that she actually opted to stay and watch them stitch it.

"Yes, I'm fine," he replied with little emotion, although he subconsciously flexed his hand several times. "Did you get a hold of the guys?"

"Yeah, they said they'd meet us outside the abandoned building tomorrow morning. Something about no electric and it getting dark soon. They intend to spend the evening questioning patrons at the tavern."

Slade snorted a soft laugh. "I'm sure that's the reason," he announced with little enthusiasm. "That's code for 'have a few drinks'." He tenderly flexed his hand. "Not a bad idea, considering how this day has gone."

"I think I'd rather keep my wits about me," she remarked then shivered subconsciously. "If the Pen Pal is some homeless man, how does he meet his victims?"

"He's not a homeless man," Slade insisted. "He's very clever and twice as resourceful. He was probably hanging around the theater for days watching the girl. Acting the part of a homeless man allowed him access to the building." He then frowned and groaned softly with defeat. "He's been known to pick up his victims in nightclubs and bars as well. I'd be willing to bet he's charming and sophisticated." He cast a look at her while raising his brows. "Monsters seldom appear frightening on the surface."

They approached Slade's car.

"That's comforting," Jolynn muttered then appeared curious. "Are you suggesting Gillian knew him prior to her abduction? Do you honestly think he was hanging around watching and signaling her out?"

"I'm confident in that theory," Slade informed her as they stopped by his car. "You told me that she spent several evenings a week at bars and nightclubs. She very easily could have socialized with him on more than one occasion."

"That's moderately frightening," Jolynn announced and sank into thought. "I've been out with her once or twice. I mean, there's a chance I've actually seen this guy before. I could possibly recognize him if I saw him again." She hesitated then shook her head. "It doesn't add up though. Even without touching him, I'd think a guy like that would have given me some sort of bad vibe though."

"Maybe he never approached her," Slade offered. "Maybe he wasn't there on nights you'd gone along. I'm not 100% sure on anything right now." He opened the passenger side door for her. "We need to stop at my hotel for a change of clothing. I'll pick up a few things and remain with you at your apartment."

Although she wasn't sure how she felt about Slade practically moving in with her, Jolynn was grateful to hear he intended to change out of his bloody shirt. She didn't want the constant reminder of his near miss. The images in her mind were already enough of a reminder.

"Hopefully, you'll get some inspiration at the warehouse tomorrow morning," Slade remarked then sighed with defeat. "We're coming up empty-handed and time is running short."

Chapter Twenty-four

The warehouse still contained police line surrounding it to keep out trespassers and nosy neighbors. By the time Slade, Jolynn, and the team reached the warehouse, it was already late Sunday morning. Within the creepy, abandoned structure, most of the blood on the walls and the chalk outline on the floor remained. Slade entered beneath the police line across the door to the main work floor. He casually placed his hands in his pockets and looked around as the rest of his team entered behind him. Slade eyed his men then looked back at the doorway with some bewilderment. Jolynn wasn't behind them. She was nowhere to be found. Slade walked back to the entrance and peered into the dingy corridor. He saw Jolynn standing frozen just outside the door staring at the yellow tape.

"Are you coming inside?" Slade asked while studying her. "It's okay."

A moment passed before Jolynn slowly entered, ducking beneath the police line. She looked around the massive room and immediately saw flashes of the gruesome murder scene, blood on the walls and floor, and the butchered woman lying naked with unusual words carved into her flesh. Jolynn listened to the woman's chilling scream and the fear she felt leading up to that moment. Jolynn suddenly looked around with fear frozen on her face. She could hear satanic whispers all around her followed by more traumatic screams. Jolynn barely had time to gasp as she turned abruptly and headed for the doorway, roughly colliding with Slade, who had purposely gotten in her path to keep her from leaving. Slade caught her by her arms to keep her from falling from their hard collision. Jolynn saw images of Slade casually walking away from a building as it exploded behind him. She again saw the dead woman with him, as she had been in life, laughing during a happier time.

The image immediately morphed into the young woman lying in her casket. Jolynn's eyes met Slade's with a horrified expression, telling him the horrors she'd seen. Before he had a chance to release her, Jolynn saw an image of Slade sitting on the kitchen floor with his head in his hands and piles of broken dishes scattered everywhere. It immediately morphed back into the image she'd seen that morning of Slade with the woman's blood on his hands. Jolynn pulled away from him as he simultaneously released her. She darted past him and hurried from the room. Slade's men stared after her with surprise to her overreaction.

"What was that?" Rush asked with some surprise and unlimited annoyance.

"Psychic overload," Slade muttered in response. "Why don't you guys wait here? Have a look around, and see if there's anything we missed last time." He drew a deep breath and held it. "I'll need a few minutes alone with her."

"This is a bad idea, Slade," Carl announced while shaking his head. "She's going to slow us down if she can't get her emotions under control."

"It's her emotions that could finally lead us to the bastard," Slade informed Carl matter-of-fact. "She has an emotional attachment to the third girl. She's our best hope of finding her friend before it's too late. She'll pull it together." He fidgeted slightly and motioned to the guys. "Just wait here."

Slade hurried from the room after Jolynn. Rush casually walked across the warehouse and observed the chalk outline as well as the remaining bloodstains with little emotion. Baxter and Carl pulled up gruesome crime scene photos on their portable electronic device and attempted to place the photos with their actual locations within the warehouse. It was doubtful they'd missed anything on their first trip out, but it was worth revisiting the crime scene, considering the extra time they seemed to have suddenly.

"What's up with Slade and this psycho woman," Baxter finally asked without looking at the others and kept his attention focused on the crime scene photos.

"Baxter--" Wilson snarled, silently threatening him.

Baxter shrugged without care and looked at the blood remaining on the walls. "She's really out there," he announced then returned Carl's portable tablet by slapping it hard against his chest. He glared at Wilson. "Even you with your weakness for the damsel in distress type has to admit that there's something seriously wrong with that girl."

Wilson glared his disapproval but despite his steely physique, he didn't call Baxter on his insult. "I'm sure Slade knows what he's doing," Wilson muttered under his breath.

"I'm with Baxter," Carl remarked with little concern for keeping his voice down. "Bringing a woman in on our mission was a bad idea, especially someone unstable like that." He looked at his teammates and pushed his glasses back onto the bridge of his nose. "How are we ever going to catch this guy if Slade's spending all his time coddling that girl?"

"It's obvious Slade has the hots for her," Baxter remarked while holding back his chuckle.

"Slade?" Rush suddenly scoffed and eyed the brawny man. "You must be joking. Slade is completely obsessed with the Pen Pal. He's not going to let some woman stand in his way." He offered an evil, twisted smirk. "Unlike you, Baxter, the rest of us don't think with our dicks. His only interest in her is how close she can get him to that fucker."

Wilson hesitated and stared at something lying on the floor near the chalk outline. He looked at the tiny fragment of what appeared to be white plastic, examined it closely, and then stuck it in an evidence bag.

"There's no denying she's quite attractive," Wilson muttered while studying the fragment in the bag then realized he'd made his comment out loud.

Rush approached Wilson to see what he had discovered and eyed the fragment through the bag as well.

Carl glared his disapproval at Wilson and then indicated Rush. "You're almost as bad as he is," he announced boldly.

"What did you find?" Rush asked, uncertain what to make of the fragment.

"Maybe nothing," Wilson replied. "Looks like a piece of tooth, but I'm sure it's some man-made material."

Baxter eyed Carl, casually leaned on his shoulder, and attempted to keep a straight face. "You know what the problem is, don't you?"

Carl glanced at Baxter who towered over him by almost eight inches and awaited the response he already knew was coming, indicated by the cheap grin plastered on his face.

"Wilson and Slade don't take the time to get laid once in a while," Baxter casually announced while attempting to play it straight, although his grin gave him away. "Makes them emotionally unstable."

Wilson turned to face Baxter and frowned his limited patience with the muscular man. "You're a real prick, Baxter." His eyes narrowed while staring him down. "I don't know how you can even think about sex after all the shit we've seen. Show a little respect for once."

Baxter removed his arm from Carl's shoulder and smirked while eyeing his teammate. "Maybe you're just a little too sensitive for this type of work."

"Too sensitive?" Wilson suddenly lashed back with a wild look in his dark eyes. "We're hunting a sexually repressed killer who gets his jollies from butchering innocent women. If you can't feel even one ounce of sympathy for what those poor women went through, you need to resign from the human race."

"Taking this a little personally, aren't you?" Baxter suddenly demanded. "What is this? Two minutes around Slade's little girlfriend and everyone's going limp?"

Wilson sneered and shook his head with disgust while attempting to hold back his hostility. It didn't work. Wilson lunged for Baxter, despite his superior build. Rush jumped between them and interceded, holding Wilson back.

"He's baiting you, Wilson," Rush remarked with little emotion. "Don't sink to his level."

Wilson allowed his large shoulders to sage with defeat, although it was clear the feud was far from over. Baxter chuckled softly, mocking his teammate.

"You could learn a lesson or two from Rush," Baxter teased while folding his arms across his muscular chest. "You need to separate yourself from it and just do your job."

Rush smirked at Baxter and nodded in silent agreement. Without even breaking his smile, Rush punched him in the mouth. Despite his size, Baxter was thrown back several steps. He held his bleeding mouth then looked at Rush with surprise. Rush maintained his evil smirk.

"Just doing my job, Baxter," Rush announced almost cheerfully. "Consider me an avenging angel. We were hired because the woman our boss loved was murdered by a psycho killer. We're here for the victims; not our egos." He tilted his head and raised a cocky brow. "Is that clear?"

Baxter sneered, slung the blood from his hand, and reluctantly nodded.

"I'm glad we finally see things eye-to-eye," Rush announced while grinning. "I'd hate for us to have a problem."

Chapter Twenty-five

Jolynn stood near the exit door facing the wall with her hands braced against it as her head hung down. She panted softly while attempting to slow her heart rate. She felt as if someone had torn out her heart, and she was unable to catch her breath. Slade slowly approached her from behind, keeping his hands securely in his pockets to avoid touching her. Without a word, he leaned his back to the wall near her and avoided looking at her.

"I told you it wouldn't be pleasant, Jolynn," Slade gently reminded her. "You need to separate yourself from it for Gillian's sake." He hesitated and searched for something to say that would help. "What happened in that room isn't uncommon. This is what he does, what he will continue to do if we don't stop him. We need to find him in order to save your friend."

She continued to pant softly but couldn't force herself to move. "He's approximately six-foot tall, about one hundred and eighty pounds, and moderately muscular." She slowly forced herself to turn and look at him. "His canine teeth are filed to points, which he uses to rip their throats out while they're still alive." Jolynn inhaled deeply and choked on the words coming from her mouth.

Slade's expression suddenly dropped at the enormous amount of detail she must've received in mere seconds. "The sick bastard drinks their blood while it's still warm. He must think he's some sort of vampire." She suddenly shuddered and insecurely rubbed her chilled arms. "He's not alone."

"What?" Slade suddenly gasped.

"Demons," she replied softly and tried to keep her body from trembling. "Those women are human sacrifices to feed the demons he worships."

Slade shook his head while straightening and putting on a brave front. He could pretend all he wanted, but Jolynn knew her words cut through him.

"I don't believe in demons," he proudly informed her.

"*They* don't care if you do or not."

Slade twitched slightly but resumed his calm demeanor. "He's just a man," he announced firmly. "Sick and twisted, but still just a man." He studied her a brief moment and attempted to sound comforting. "Will you come back to the room and see what else you can find?"

"Don't make me go back in there. There's nothing in that room that will help," Jolynn insisted while vigorously shaking her head. "What happened in there is all about death and torture. Seeing what he did to that poor girl--" She drew a deep, shaken breath. "*Reliving* what he did to that girl isn't going to help us find him or Gillian. It's all in the past. You don't need me to tell you what you already know."

Slade looked into her eyes and forced a tiny, reassuring smile. "I won't make you do anything you're uncomfortable with," he gently informed her. "I don't mean to be cold and callus, Jolynn. I'm sorry to admit, after a while it just becomes second nature."

"Only if you allow it." Jolynn proudly straightened, drew a deep breath, and hid her fearful emotions. "You don't need to worry about me. I don't want to slow you down. All that matters is finding Gillian."

"If you don't think there's anything else here that will help then we need to investigate somewhere else," Slade boldly remarked. "The guys can finish their search without us." He studied Jolynn a moment and appeared curious. "Would visiting the home of victim number two be of any use? There's a good chance she's still alive. We still have a chance to save her. Her parents live near here just on the edge of town. Perhaps you can establish a connection to her." He fidgeted slightly. "If we find her, it might lead us to Gillian and the Pen Pal."

Jolynn nodded and attempted a smile. "I think you're right," she replied. "If I can establish a connection to her, we may be able to find her."

Slade studied her a moment longer and smiled gently. "Are you sure you're feeling well enough?"

She eyed him suspiciously and tilted her head. "Why are you suddenly being so nice?" she asked. "What happened to that rude man I met in medical records?"

"Being rude keeps people at a distance," he informed her. "It keeps them from liking me."

She hid her smile. "We can't have that."

"I've learned to live a guarded life. Any distraction could be fatal," he announced then hesitated while staring into her eyes. "Especially when she's very attractive."

Jolynn was surprised by the comment then hid her smile. "Then don't be distracted," she gently replied. "I'd hate to see anything happen to you."

They stared into one another's eyes a moment longer. Slade was first to slip out of his misguided thoughts. He managed a smile and extended his hand toward the door near her.

"Shall we?"

Jolynn smiled warmly and slipped out the door. Slade hesitated, groaned softly, and followed after her.

Chapter Twenty-six

Beth Riesler's house was located a few miles outside Linville just along the border of River Run, a small farming community. The cute little split-level house belonging to Beth's parents came complete with a traditional, white picket fence and assorted toys on the lawn. The flowerbed was colorful with plenty of blooming flowers despite the many overgrown weeds attempting to choke them out. Slade's black town car was parked out front even though there was plenty of room behind the slightly used SUV with more than its share of dents, scratches, and dings.

Slade and Jolynn were welcomed into the modest split-level home by Beth's worried looking mother. Mrs. Riesler looked almost haggard from being put through hell after her daughter's disappearance. She appeared restless and exhausted, indicated by the dark circles under her weary eyes. She dressed slightly frumpy, indicating the high level of her recent depression.

"I'm so glad you came by, Agent Slade," Mrs. Riesler announced while clinging insecurely to her arms within her oversized sweater. "No one seems to have any information on my daughter's disappearance."

"We're doing everything we can, I assure you," Slade gently informed her.

"It's reassuring just having you stop by again," she said while attempting to relax. "At least I feel as if someone's actually doing something."

"This is Jolynn Raynard," Slade announced while indicating Jolynn. "She's a psychic consultant and our best lead so far."

"It's a pleasure to meet you," Mrs. Riesler greeted Jolynn, nearly choking on her words. "I'll do whatever it takes to help bring my daughter back alive."

"I'd like to take Miss Raynard to your daughter's bedroom," Slade informed the grieving woman. "She needs to establish a connection with her. Maybe allow her something small and personal belonging to Beth that she can take with her."

"Oh, anything. You can show yourselves to her room. You know where it is," Mrs. Riesler announced practically coming to life before their eyes. "I'll get you her favorite necklace. It's in my room."

Mrs. Riesler hurried from the room with a renewed sense of hope. Slade guided Jolynn up the stairs and along the second floor hall, knowing his way from a previous visit.

"I don't like this," Jolynn whispered, "deceiving her."

"If it brings her daughter back, she won't care if we're from another planet."

Slade guided Jolynn into the nearby bedroom, which was left exactly as Beth had left it. The young woman's bedroom was feminine looking and still decorated from when Beth was a younger girl. Jolynn walked around the room and focused on certain items that seemed to catch her attention. Beth's mother entered the room with renewed enthusiasm then saw Jolynn pick up a glass angel. Mrs. Riesler suddenly stopped in the doorway and watched Jolynn gently caress the angel. Beth's mother clutched the necklace in her hand and held it to her chest while holding her breath. Obviously, the angel held some significance to the woman. Jolynn stared at the glass angel a long moment, watching light dancing off its wings. She then saw a flash of Beth bound and gagged in a room filled with candles and bloody writing along the walls. Jolynn held back her emotions to keep from losing the image.

"That's her favorite," Mrs. Riesler announced softly. "It was a gift from her grandmother just before she died."

Jolynn continued to stare at the glass angel, blocking out the woman's voice. She could hear Beth sobbing among the sound of low chanting. The chanting was from an evil voice. Beth was terrified of the man shrouded in darkness. Jolynn heard a train whistle in the background. Light glistened off the blade of a knife. It delicately carved something into her chest. Beth screamed with pain and horror beneath the gag. Jolynn suddenly gasped, the glass angel slipping from her hand and shattering on the floor. Beth's mother let out a startled scream and jumped with surprise. Slade ran to Jolynn's side, reaching to touch her but reconsidered and pulled back. He couldn't risk tainting her vision.

"Jolynn, what did you see?" Slade asked with urgency in his tone.

Jolynn turned to face him, the horror showing in her eyes. "I saw her," she gasped. "I heard a train."

Slade looked at Beth's mother in silent question. Mrs. Riesler stared at Jolynn as if she were ready to jump from her skin then focused her attention on Slade.

"There's a train on the other side of town in River Run," Mrs. Riesler quickly informed them while urgently pointing. "It's just past River Run Medical Center."

"Any abandoned buildings?" he pressed.

"Uh, there's the old train station, a factory, and a house along that track," she responded in rushed speech.

Without hesitation, Jolynn snatched the locket from Mrs. Riesler and held it tightly in her hand, shutting her eyes. Slade removed his cell phone and hit a single button. The call was immediately answered.

"Carl, take the van to the railroad on the far side of town. Check out the abandoned house," he announced into his cell phone while pacing the small bedroom. "Send Wilson to the old factory. Jolynn and I are going to the old train station." He was silent while listening to his response then turned hostile. "I don't care *how*. Steal a car if you have too!"

Slade disconnected the call and returned his attention to Jolynn as she clutched the locket. Beth's mother nervously wrenched her fingers together while watching in silence. Jolynn kept her eyes closed and trembled slightly, grasping the locket so tight her knuckles turned white.

"It's bright," Jolynn gasped softly. "I'm seeing broken stained glass windows. There's an old billboard."

"It's the train station," Beth's mother proclaimed.

Slade sprang into action and bolted for the bedroom door. He suddenly stopped and looked back. "Jolynn--now!"

His sharp words startled her, causing her eyes to open. She turned and ran after Slade, leaving Mrs. Riesler alone in the room both frazzled and anxious.

✝

*B*eth lay on the wooden bench within the train station with her eyes closed. Her hands remained tied and the duct tape was securely across her mouth. Candlelight flickered within the dimly lit waiting area. A shadow loomed over her, waking her from her dazed state. Her eyes widened as she stared with horror at the figure standing over her and attempted to scream through the duct tape.

Chapter Twenty-seven

Slade drove his town car at high speeds along the back road on the edge of town while following the railroad tracks. He held his cell phone to his ear in his free hand while attempting to keep his car on the road.

"No, I want everyone at the train station!"

Jolynn remained quietly seated in the front passenger seat while clutching Beth's locket. She seemed to be in another world where Slade's radical driving and near misses with parked cars didn't touch her. The sound of a car's horn jolted her back into reality. She opened her eyes just in time to witness Slade nearly hitting another car. Jolynn screamed in response and clutched the door handle. Slade tossed the cell phone over his shoulder into the backseat and placed both hands on the wheel to keep from losing control of the car. Jolynn couldn't take her eyes off the road and the high-speed driving as her stomach and heart seemed to meet in her abdomen.

A brilliant light suddenly flashed in front of Jolynn's eyes, dragging her into another vision unlike any she'd ever had before. She gasped barely able to catch her breath. She no longer saw the road or was even aware she was in Slade's car. She saw a man's unnaturally sharpened teeth penetrating Beth's throat. Beth muffled a scream as blood erupted from her neck while the teeth tore through her flesh. Jolynn's eyes suddenly opened with horror and fear as she clutched her pounding head, feeling as if her world was spinning. She screamed hysterically and repeatedly slammed her fist clutching the locket against the passenger side window as if fighting off some unseen attacker.

Slade's reaction was that of shock as he grabbed her hand, attempting to stop her thrashing fist from striking the already cracked and bloodied window. Images from Slade's past struck like lightning through Jolynn's mind. She witnessed Slade casting stacks of china from the kitchen cupboards, shattering as they struck the floor. She saw burning buildings and rapidly flashing images of mutilated women. Jolynn screamed hysterically while fighting him, the images, and Beth's phantom screams. Slade caught an image of what lie ahead of him in the road and released her arm in an attempt to control the car, but it was too late.

Slade's car barreled through the closed gates to the abandoned train station. The tires squealed as the car skidded into a flying half circle and slammed into the side of the building. Jolynn's head hit the already cracked side window upon impact. Slade's airbag exploded then fizzled out. For a moment, he was slumped in his seat looking dazed. He slowly lifted his head and looked at Jolynn. Her eyes were closed as blood streaked her head resting against the headrest. Slade hurriedly removed his seatbelt and hovered over her a moment with a look of concern. He considered his next move only a brief moment before deciding to risk touching her.

"Jolynn?" he gasped while gently nudging her. "Jo, wake up."

Her eyes slowly rolled opened as she attempted to focus on him, clearly disoriented. Her expression dropped as she suddenly realized where she was and what had happened.

"Get that bastard," she gasped without forethought.

He hesitated only a moment while staring at her as if debating his next move. He cursed softly, removed his semiautomatic, and bolted from the car.

†

Slade cautiously entered the train station with his gun clutched firmly in his hand. The old passenger waiting area was filled with dust covered benches and tables. Beth lay naked on one of the nearby benches. Her eyes remained open and her throat had been torn out, leaving her covered in fresh blood. She only had one symbol carved into her chest but none along the remainder of her body as with the other victims. He was unable to finish his ritual, which meant he was still within the building. It also meant he was possibly nearby. Slade looked around the dirty, cluttered station then spotted the bathroom just a few yards away. He quickly straightened and headed toward the bathroom.

A dark figure suddenly leaped from the shadows and tackled Slade to the floor, knocking the wind from him as well as his gun. Slade's gun slid across the hard floor and into the darkness. Slade finally got his first good look at the Pen Pal. He wore a zombie clown mask, which was covered in fresh blood down the chin and the front of his shirt. The blood of his latest victim was a grim reminder that he was a monster. Despite the force of the impact, Slade managed to knock the knife from the killer's hand. The Pen Pal punched Slade in the face, momentarily stunning him, and giving him enough time to leap to his feet and for the discarded knife. Slade pulled himself to his feet and kicked the Pen Pal in the face as he reached for the knife. The Pen Pal staggered back a step, as if barely even fazed then glared at Slade. His sharply filed, bloodstained teeth were bared as he snarled like a wild beast. The crazed man leaped for Slade.

Slade spun into a high roundhouse kick and caught the Pen Pal in the face. The killer staggered back several feet and struck the wall but not nearly hard enough to stun him longer than a moment. He growled and once more leaped for Slade. Slade jumped onto a wooden bench and out of his path. The Pen Pal struck the edge of the bench with force then spun and darted for his discarded knife. Slade leaped from the bench and landed on the Pen Pal's back, riding him to the floor. Slade toppled off the killer and rolled several feet across the floor. The Pen Pal snatched his decorative dagger as Slade scrambled for his nearby gun. Slade grabbed the gun and whirled onto his backside, prepared to fire.

The Pen Pal was gone! The door behind the ticket counter fell back into place. Slade ran for the door, threw it open, and aimed his gun into the next room. The large room was dimly lit and cluttered with old furniture. He could have been hiding within any corner. Slade slowly entered the room and looked around, being cautious of the dark corners.   The slaughtered remains of what was probably once a homeless man were scattered along the floor. Tattered, dirty clothes, puddles of dried blood, and chunks of flesh were all that remained of the unfortunate man who had undoubtedly been living in the train station at the time.   Slade cringed from the foul smell of decaying flesh and cautiously crossed the dimly lit room.

Chapter Twenty-eight

Jolynn weakly slammed her shoulder into the passenger side door several times before the door gave loose and opened with a grinding creak. She slowly got out of the car and nearly fell to the cracked pavement overgrown with weeds. She staggered a few steps toward the damaged front of the car, which was smashed into the side of the building, and attempted to focus on the main entrance she was certain Slade had gone through. She had no idea how long he'd been gone, and her concern for him was growing with each passing second. Something commanded her to look at the locket clenched in her severely scraped and bleeding hand. Jolynn realized Beth was dead. They had been too late. She clutched her bleeding head a moment, held back her sobs, and then cried out with anger as she threw the locket into the car through the open passenger door.

She leaned on the crinkled hood not far from the open door and held her bleeding head a moment longer. Despite her throbbing head and extreme dizziness, her anger at herself was greater than any pain she was experiencing from the accident. She let Beth down. If she couldn't save Beth, what made her think she'd ever be able to save Gillian? The thought of Gillian dying because of her was more than she could bear. It would be a gruesome death she'd undoubtedly witness in her visions as it happened. She couldn't let that happen. She stifled her sniff and straightened with renewed concern for Slade. His men still hadn't arrived, and he was all alone inside the abandoned train station with the serial killer. Jolynn then remembered Slade's cell phone was in the backseat of the car. She needed to find it and call for backup. Jolynn turned toward the open car door and came face-to-face with the Pen Pal.

The zombie clown mask was covered with fresh blood from his recent kill, and she could see his sharpened teeth stained with Beth's blood. Jolynn fixated on the blood that covered the chin of his mask and ran down his neck to the front of his shirt. For a moment, she relived Beth's dying moment in horrifying detail. It was the only vision she got from the frightening killer. Jolynn returned to reality and saw the Pen Pal raising his decorative dagger about to strike it down upon her. She jumped backwards, striking the car. Despite her dizziness, Jolynn leaped out of the way. The decorative dagger and his hand smashed through the side passenger window. Jolynn turned to make her escape while the Pen Pal struggled to free his hand from the glass.

She suddenly stopped and considered the worst idea in a long history of bad ideas. She turned toward the trapped, struggling psychopath and grabbed ahold of his free left wrist. He was clearly surprised by her odd action but wasted little time attempting to grab onto her while yanking his right hand with the knife free from the broken window. Despite the horrifying position she'd put herself into, she refused to let go. Jolynn saw hundreds of flashes involving gruesome murders, terrified women being butchered, decayed bodies, abandoned buildings with bloody symbols, and incredible violence she could barely fathom. The Pen Pal slashed at her with the dagger. She saw the dagger coming at her almost as if in slow motion. As she released him and jumped to the side, the dagger scratched her forearm. Her eyes strayed to his pendant necklace and the familiar symbol in handmade silver. It called to her.

All she could think about was her inability to save Beth and her friend's uncertain fate. With every ounce of emotion and courage left within her, Jolynn rammed her knee into his groin. He flinched enough to stop the knife from a second strike but wasn't nearly as fazed as he should have been. Jolynn snatched his pendant necklace and pulled with all her strength and most of her body. The leather cord snapped, causing her to fall to the ground. Slade appeared from another entrance at the far end of the station and stared with horror at the unfolding situation. The Pen Pal grasped the dagger in both hands and was about to plunge it into her where she lie helpless on the pavement.

Slade aimed and fired his gun from a distance. Although the bullet was nearly silent, it made a distinctive sound as it ricocheted off the car near the Pen Pal's head, just missing his masked face. Jolynn rolled out of the way, even though the killer was no longer interested in stabbing her. The Pen Pal now focused his attention on Slade, who was running toward him with his gun aimed, prepared to fire again. The killer dived into Slade's car, threw it into reverse, and burned-out backwards away from the building. Jolynn covered her face as Slade repeatedly fired his weapon, hitting the car as it took off for the open gate. The black van swerved to miss Slade's car and slammed into the steel fence. Slade ran to Jolynn and fell to her side. He made a motion to help her but held back, uncertain if he should touch her or not.

"What the hell were you doing?" he cried out in anger, although he was clearly concerned for her. "You nearly got yourself killed!"

Jolynn slowly sat up to reveal the pendant necklace clutched in her hand and offered a tiny smile while panting. "Getting directions."

Slade stared at the pendant with surprise then smirked and shook his head. "What *am* I going to do with you?"

Jolynn's smile faded as she placed her hand to her head. "Uh, I don't feel so good--"

Slade lunged for her as she started to fall backwards and caught her. Jolynn's eyes rolled shut as she slipped into unconsciousness.

Chapter Twenty-nine

The damaged black van parked along a backstretch of road boarding Linville and River Run. The old farmhouse was located in an overgrown field and was barely visible from the back road. It was close to the railroad tracks and only half a mile from the abandoned railroad station. Slade's team knew it was a long shot that Gillian was being held in an area so close to where Beth had been held, but it was worth checking out. The four men checked the magazines in their firearms, replaced them to their shoulder holsters, and filed out of the van. They placed their transmitters into their ears and attached them to the cell phones clipped onto their belts. All four hurried along the old driveway and up to the house while keeping out of sight.

"We'll take the back," Carl informed Wilson and Rush. "You two take the front."

Wilson and Rush nodded and waited for Carl and Baxter to make their way around to the back of the dilapidated old house before making their approach to the front. Wilson was the first to step onto the rickety, old porch. It creaked loudly as if it would snap beneath his weight. When he got the 'all clear' from Carl and

Baxter at the back door, he swiftly kicked the door in without missing a stride. Wilson and Rush entered like a swat team, filing in quickly with their guns drawn. Carl and Baxter could be heard entering from the back as well. The first floor hallway was in disrepair with peeling paint and holes in the plaster. Rush and Wilson cautiously scaled the rickety, old stairs with broken railing and missing boards on the steps. Despite their caution, the creaking from the old steps was almost deafening.

✝

*B*axter and Carl entered the back sitting room just off the kitchen. There were a few tattered blankets and a pillow crawling with bugs on the old, torn sofa. The remains of an unidentifiable animal were scattered along the floor near the sofa. Whatever the animal had once been, it appeared to be half-eaten, leaving bloodstained fur and day old rotting innards surrounding the broken, scattered bones. Baxter and Carl exchanged looks of disgust at the killer's leftover dinner.

"This is the place all right," Baxter muttered.

Carl touched his ear transmitter. "He's been here within the last day or two," he informed the others. "Keep alert. If we're lucky, he came back here after the train station."

"Roger that. Personally, I'm dying to run into this guy," Rush responded through his ear transmitter. "Wilson and I are on the second floor."

"Yeah, we hear you," Carl announced while looking at the ceiling. The old boards on the second floor groaned loudly above them. "Sounds like you're about to fall through the floor." He then looked at Baxter, who continued to stare at the half-eaten animal and grimaced. "Baxter and I will continue our search for the girl down here."

✝

*W*ilson opened the first bedroom door on the right while Rush checked out the room to the left. Wilson jumped into the doorway with his gun aimed, but the room was empty except for a tattered, old blanket. He looked around the empty room and immediately noted the writing in blood on the walls. He frowned his disappointment then tapped his ear transmitter.

"Whatever happened here," Wilson announced gruffly, "we missed it."

He approached the tattered blanket not far from the bedroom door and gave it a slight kick with his foot. A credit card lay on the floor. Wilson appeared curious as he picked up the card and eyed the name embossed on it. Gillian Foxwood. He groaned softly and again tapped his ear transmitter.

"Guys," he announced with a defeated sigh. "We have confirmation that the girl was being held here. I found her credit card. Looks tattered. I think she tried to pop the bedroom door lock."

"Bag it," Rush announced over Wilson's transmitter. "We should notify Slade right away. We'll need to sweep the house and see if there's anything to indicate where he may have taken her."

"I'll notify Slade," Wilson responded with defeat. He then removed his cell phone from his belt clip, pressed a number on speed dial, and waited for Slade to answer.

†

River Run Medical Center was small and cozy for a country hospital. The emergency waiting room was nearly empty that evening except for Slade and another man, who resembled a young farmer. Unlike Slade, the farmer was particularly calm and seemed to enjoy his crossword puzzle from that morning's paper. Slade paced the waiting area while nervously running his fingers through his hair. The farmer watched him pace then finally sat forward and offered a reassuring smile.

"Your first one?" the farmer asked.

Slade looked at the man and appeared puzzled. "Excuse me?" he asked.

"Most fellas are nervous the first time," the farmer informed him in a calm tone. "This is our sixth. After the third, they pretty much crawl out on their own."

Slade stared with some surprise at the farmer who had to be only in his late twenties. He then realized what the young farmer had been speculating as his reason for the hospital visit. Slade's cell phone rang from within his jacket pocket, sparing him further conversation on childbirth. He grabbed his phone from his pocket and eagerly answered it.

"Yeah?"

A nurse at the front desk eyed him and the cell phone. "Sir, you'll have to use that outside," she informed him. "Cell phones aren't permitted--"

Slade didn't give her a chance to finish before hurrying to the emergency room doors and stepping into the outer cove. He listened to his man on the other end.

"We have evidence that our friend had been at the abandoned house not far from the train station," Wilson announced through the phone. "I found a credit card with our girl's name on it. She was here, but he must have moved her after his near miss at the train station."

Slade cursed softly under his breath and continued to pace. "Damn it," he growled softly then nervously looked around. "Uh, I can't leave here. Jolynn's still being evaluated. She hasn't regained consciousness yet."

"After taking on our guy like that, she's lucky to be alive," Wilson grumbled from the other end. "We'll finish sweeping the house, but I think we've missed him. There's no telling where he's heading now."

"I understand," Slade remarked. "I'll have Jolynn check the house as soon as she's able."

"Should we bring the credit card to the hospital?" Wilson asked. "Maybe she can get something from it that can help us tonight."

"No. Jolynn's been through enough for one day," Slade quickly replied. "They won't even let me in to see her. Just, uh, finish your sweep. I'll call you in the morning."

There was an odd silence from Wilson's end. "Should we let you know what else turns up?"

Slade glanced back at the hospital desk from where he stood in the alcove. A familiar nurse approached the desk from the back. Slade twitched with concern.

"No--no. I, uh, really have to go," Slade announced. "I'll call you later."

Slade disconnected the call before Wilson could respond and hurried back inside to the desk and the nurses. He placed his hands on the desk and looked at the second nurse.

"The young lady I brought in earlier--how's she doing?" he asked in a rushed tone. He attempted to sound calm but failed miserably.

"She has a mild concussion," the nurse informed him. "She's in and out, but she's going to be fine. The doctor may want to keep her for observation."

"Can I see her?"

"Are you her husband?" she questioned skeptically while eying him.

"Yes," Slade replied without hesitation.

"I'll check with the doctor," she informed him. "Please wait here."

Slade watched her leave then continued to pace the small waiting room. He glanced at the young farmer, who remained perfectly calm while waiting for his wife to give birth. The young man, although remarkably clueless, watched Slade pace with obvious humor, still believing he was awaiting his own baby's birth. Slade groaned softly and avoided looking at the young man to prevent further conversation. He then hesitated, met the young man's gaze, and gave him a baffled look.

"Six kids?" Slade suddenly asked, as if the earlier conversation finally sank in.

Chapter Thirty

Sheriff Gruber's police cruiser pulled up behind the black van where it was parked just down the road from the abandoned house. Having been in near shambles for years, the house itself was practically invisible to most people who lived in the area. Sheriff Gruber got out of the police car, adjusted his holster beneath his excessively round girth, and approached the van. He checked the license plate then headed for the driver's side door. When he didn't see a driver, he rounded the van and approached the back sliding door on the passenger side. Being the door was slightly ajar; he pulled the door open the rest of the way and peered inside.

The state of the art surveillance system and the overwhelming elegance of the van's interior surprised the country cop. He pushed his hat back on his head and rested his thumbs inside his holster while studying the technology within the van.

"What the hell--?" he muttered, puzzled by the sight of such sophisticated equipment in his little town.

Sheriff Gruber was about to crawl inside the van to give it a closer inspection when his radio chirped from his hip. He reached for his radio while turning his head and caught a glimpse of a zombie clown standing behind him.

"What the--?"

As he turned to see who or what was behind him, he only saw the decorative dagger plunging downward before his face. Gruber cried out in horror while fumbling for his gun.

†

Jolynn watched dozens of images play out within her dreams. It was a jumble of men and women running around in lab coats and scrub uniforms. Some were performing CPR while annoying high-pitched sounds interrupted her moderately relaxed mood. Others were flirting with their peers, some even taking it a step beyond that. She saw orderlies pushing sick patients around in their wheelchairs while telling them corny jokes to lighten the mood. Jolynn wasn't sure where she was, since she seemed to have no body. She could hear voices speaking over her, yet she was witnessing professional and personal scenes in the lives of these people she didn't know. The jumble of images finally faded, leaving just one woman left in her subconscious. Her only vision allowed her to watch the young woman drenched in sweat lying in her hospital bed as the doctor handed her the tiny, swaddled baby. The woman shed tears of joy while cuddling her newborn.

"I've waited a long time to meet you, baby Rose," the woman whispered to the softly crying baby.

Another flash showed the unborn baby on the ultrasound monitor. Jolynn listened to the sound of the baby's heart beating while the mother clutched the father's hand and sobbed tears of joy. Jolynn felt oddly relaxed at that moment. Nothing else seemed to matter. She heard voices speaking over her as the sound of the baby's heartbeat faded into her subconscious. Jolynn slowly opened her eyes to a nearly blinding light. As she attempted to look around, she realized she was in a small examination room undoubtedly in some hospital's emergency room. She once again heard the baby's heart beating as the young nurse examined the sutured cut on her arm. She recognized the nurse as the woman holding the baby in her vision. The nurse smiled sympathetically at Jolynn while wrapping her sutured arm.

"I'm glad to see you finally decided to join us," the nurse announced cheerfully and taped the wrappings over her injury to hold them in place.

"Did I pass out?" Jolynn softly asked.

"Yes, you've been unconscious nearly an hour," the nurse informed her. "You were in a car accident. Do you remember what happened?"

Jolynn recalled the incident in frightening clarity. "Yeah, I'm driving next time," she muttered.

The nurse smiled and patted her hand. "I think you should too."

As the nurse took her pulse, Jolynn's eyes strayed to the woman's toned, flattened abdomen. She watched images of the tiny fetus sleeping peacefully. The nurse studied the fixated look on Jolynn's face then offered a warm smile.

"Your husband is worried," the nurse cheerfully informed her. "Would you like to see him?"

Jolynn appeared confused by her comment and met her gaze. Nothing appeared to register. She didn't remember being married, but she wasn't feeling strong enough to argue about it.

"I guess so," Jolynn replied, although remaining puzzled. As the nurse squeezed her hand, Jolynn again listened to the baby's heart beating. The sound was comforting. She met the nurse's gaze and managed her best smile despite her disorientation. "Is this your first baby?"

The nurse hesitated and stared at Jolynn with a look of surprise followed by a near shattering expression.

"Baby? I, uh, don't have a baby," the nurse informed her and stifled the tears swelling in her eyes. "We tried for the longest time, but we gave up."

Jolynn felt her weary mind slipping in and out of consciousness. She was nearly as tired as the little baby in the nurse's womb. Jolynn managed a smile, appreciating the tiny life she was able to watch in ultrasound flashes.

"She's going to be a redhead like her daddy," Jolynn announced as her eyes closed and a smile crossed her face. She then whispered, "Little baby Rose."

The nurse stared at Jolynn with an odd look and uncertainly released her hand. The faint sound of the baby's heartbeat left along with the nurse's touch. Jolynn immediately slipped back into consciousness, missing the sound, and glanced at the IV lines connected to her arm.

"Can you remove that line?" Jolynn softly pleaded. "I don't get along well with painkillers. They make me foggy."

The nurse continued to stare at her with her mouth partially hanging open and appeared unable to respond at first. She finally managed a smile and backed away from her bed. "I'll have to check with the doctor," the nurse replied then smiled timidly. "I'll send your husband in."

The nurse headed for the door while uncertainly looking down at her own abdomen. She gently touched her flattened belly and sank into thought. Jolynn sluggishly grabbed the tubes, removed them from her arm, and cast them aside.

Chapter Thirty-one

Not even a minute had passed before Slade entered the room with the nurse. The nurse saw the tube lying on the floor oozing liquid and immediately ran to scoop up the bag. Slade approached Jolynn while offering a warm smile. He mildly glanced at the discarded line, held back his chuckle, and appeared pleased with her alert and bold attitude.

"How are you feeling?" Slade asked then eyed the nurse at the pole.

For the nurse's benefit, he leaned over her bed and kissed Jolynn on the forehead. Jolynn saw faint and hazy flashes of Slade with his arms around the murdered woman from his past as she had been in life. They smiled and laughed together from a happier time. Jolynn stared at Slade as he once more avoided contact.

"I'll get the doctor," the nurse announced and again hurried from the room.

Slade grimaced slightly and appeared embarrassed. "They weren't going to let me in," he insisted. "I had to tell them we were married." He hesitated and studied her with some concern. "How do you feel?"

She stared at him and remained puzzled. "When did we get married?"

He snorted a soft laugh. "I see you're feeling a little too good."

"I feel like I'm drunk and hungover at the same time," Jolynn muttered. "Can we go home now?"

"We have to see what the doctor says first."

"They have me so doped up, I can't think straight," she announced in a slightly groggy tone.

"I don't need you slipping into a coma either," Slade firmly insisted.

She looked away from him and groaned. "I don't know why the hell I ever married you."

He laughed softly. "I'm sure you don't."

The young, lanky doctor entered the room with a clipboard in his hand. His eye-catching tie boldly contained cartoon characters, leaving Jolynn slightly puzzled about the doctor's seriousness. He approached her bed while studying the clipboard then met her gaze and grinned.

"I hear you're tired of us already." He then read from the clipboard. "Mild concussion. Be glad you were wearing your seat belt."

"Can I go home now?"

The doctor eyed her then looked at Slade. "We could keep her overnight for observations," he announced with a humorous grin. "You could have the guys over for poker."

"I'd rather get her home tonight, if at all possible," Slade informed the doctor.

"I suppose I could release her." The doctor smiled then playfully pointed his pen at him in a suggestive manner. "There can be hanky," he teased, "but absolutely no panky for twenty-four hours."

Slade held back his humored laugh. "I think I'll manage."

"Try not to let her sleep much tonight--just in case," the doctor informed him. "If she starts feeling sick, you'll have to bring her back."

"Absolutely," Slade replied with relief. "Just send the bill to that home address."

"You've got it." He then looked at Jolynn. "Are you sure you wouldn't prefer to stay with us a little while longer?" the doctor asked then grinned. "They're serving a lovely morphine drip with just a hint of antibiotic tonight."

"I'm sure," she replied and attempted to sit up.

The doctor groaned and looked back at Slade. "She always this bullheaded?"

"Believe me, this is an improvement."

"She's going to be quite sedated for a few hours," the doctor informed him. "She's a fall risk, so don't leave her unattended. If not, you'll be bringing her back for more stitches."

The doctor and Slade shook hands. Jolynn attempted to get out of bed without waiting for assistance. The doctor eyed her, shook his head, and left the room. Jolynn fell back onto the bed with a soft, exhausted groan. Slade approached Jolynn with his hands casually in his pockets and offered a weak smile.

"One small problem, Jolynn," Slade announced with some apprehension. "You won't be able to get out of that bed by yourself, let alone walk on your own. We could either wait until the drugs wear off in a few hours, or you'll have to let me help you." His look turned serious. "In which case, you mentally rape me and throw yourself into a psychotic rage."

"They have me so high on painkillers; I won't be able to sense much anyway."

Slade appeared surprised by the response. "You mean I can touch you without being mentally and physically molested?" he teased then grinned. "This is a rare treat."

She glared demandingly at him. "Just get me the hell out of here."

Slade chuckled softly and helped her to her feet as she clung to him for support.

Chapter Thirty-two

Slade's team approached the black van parked alongside the road not far from the abandoned house. All four men appeared disgusted, indicating they'd found little more than evidence that Gillian had been held captive there, but no information on her current condition or whereabouts. The van remained parked alone on the stretch of back road. It was fortunate for them that the road was lightly traveled and their van hadn't attracted any attention where they left it abandoned. Baxter maintained a look of disgust as he marched toward the van.

"He'd better get his mind off that girl," Baxter announced as they approached the rear of the van.

"Cut him a break," Wilson muttered with defeat as he ran his fingers through his excessively short hair. "He's allowed to feel guilty that she got hurt. She took on a serial killer just to get some shred of information on her friend."

"This isn't the time or place to lose your head over some freaky chick," Baxter snapped, obviously disgusted with the entire situation. "Dealing with a nut like the Pen Pal, we can't afford to have Slade slipping up."

"He won't," Rush snarled in an intimidating tone that was meant to end the debate. Judging by Baxter's frown and ensuing silence, it worked.

All four approached the side door facing away from the road to replace their equipment. Rush slid open the side door. All four looked inside and froze simultaneously. A large pool of relatively fresh blood covered the van floor. Rush jumped away from the door and aimed his gun inside the van, although it would have done little good had someone been waiting to ambush them. The others stared at the gruesome sight, unable to move.

"Holy shit," Carl cried out.

"Is it her?" Wilson asked while peering across the back of the van to locate the body amongst the blood.

Carl removed his gun as well and slowly stepped closer to the open van door and peered inside. He looked back with a horrified expression.

"Jesus--" Carl gasped.

Baxter then looked inside and cringed. "He didn't leave the body."

All four looked around the area and soon discovered blood along the side of the road. They were equally concerned for several reasons, but the most important one was at the front of each of their minds.

"He knows we're after him," Wilson gasped with surprise and looked around the area surrounding the van as if expecting to find him hiding in the brush. "He's making a statement. He knows where to find us."

"That fucker's watching us," Rush snapped.

"We'd better call Slade," Carl remarked and reached in his pocket for his phone.

"Don't bother," Baxter muttered with irritation. "His phone's shut off."

"Then we'd better find him," Carl nearly shouted, entering panic mode. "Where does Jolynn live?"

"Slade never said," Wilson replied while attempting to remain calm.

"Great! Just great," Carl exploded. "What the hell do we do now?"

"Just remain calm," Wilson replied, taking his own advice.

"Calm?" Carl exploded while glaring at his partner with fire in his eyes. "Screw calm! It looks like he gutted someone in our van. You try to stay calm!"

"He's probably far from here by now," Rush replied while replacing his gun to his shoulder holster and seemed less rattled than the others. "Let's just get to the hotel and document the crime scene. We'll see if we can determine whose blood that is by the time Slade calls back."

They nodded in agreement. Carl rounded the van for the driver's seat while Rush and Baxter cringed as they climbed in through the side door, attempting to avoid the blood. Wilson opened the passenger side door and suddenly jumped back with a startled gasp. Sheriff Gruber's severed head was proudly displayed on the front passenger seat, his eyes open wide, and his mouth gapped as if in mid-scream.

"Fuck," Wilson cried out, throwing calm aside. "That's the sheriff! The bastard got the sheriff!"

All four men leaped out of the van and collected alongside the road. They stared at the severed head a moment then looked around for any sign of the rest of the sheriff. There wasn't any sign of his body or his cruiser.

Chapter Thirty-three

Jolynn slowly entered her apartment with Slade holding her around the waist and keeping her steady with his free hand clinging to her elbow. She remained heavily sedated and slightly dizzy from the concussion, causing her uncertainty with each step. Slade released her only a second to close and lock the apartment door behind them. Jolynn continued across the living room and bumped into the back of the loveseat. She barely even realized she'd bumped into something. Slade hurried after her and reclaimed her waist and hand to keep her steady and on course.

"I think you'd better let me help you into bed," he gently informed her. "You shouldn't be on your feet without assistance. You'll end up on the floor."

She didn't protest or comment. It was unclear if she even heard him. She obediently walked down the short hallway toward her bedroom with him as he helped keep her steady and upright. Jolynn's plain looking bedroom had very few frills with very little to indicate it was a woman's room. The bland room mildly reflected her personality. Depressing, void of hope, and lonely. Slade helped Jolynn to the simple wood framed double bed and held onto her while pulling the solid gray sheets down. Jolynn watched him as he straightened the pillows, arranging them for her comfort. A tiny smile crept across her face. Perhaps it was her imagination, but she could almost see a caring, softer side to him.

"Do you have any children, Slade?" she asked aloud even though she hadn't intended to.

He straightened and gave her an odd look. "No, why do you ask?"

"You remind me of a father putting his child to bed," she teased softly and hid her timid smile. "Almost like you've done it before."

Slade fidgeted slightly then offered an uncomfortable smile. "My mother died when my sister and I were very young," he informed her then hesitated. "My father wasn't around much, and when he was, he wasn't exactly kid friendly. So it was mostly just my sister and I."

"You took care of your sister?" She didn't mean for her words to sound so surprised, but she was having a difficult time tempering her emotions.

Slade attempted a smile but appeared uncomfortable with the topic. "I tried."

"Tried?"

He swiftly changed the subject. "Would you like me to raid your nightgown drawer?"

"I doubt anything would fit you," she gently teased, not even sure why she said it, although the comment did cause him to blush slightly, so it was worth it. "I'll sleep in my shirt and shorts. Well, what little sleep I'm allowed."

She could feel reality returning to her now. It seemed as if the painkillers were wearing off rapidly. She was grateful. Jolynn didn't like feeling foggy and out of control.

"I'll check on you a few times throughout the night," Slade announced then studied her a long moment as they stood by her bedside. A strange, hard to read smile crossed his face. He shook his head in disbelief. "I can't believe you took on that psychopath when you could've run. It was either very brave or incredibly stupid."

It was her turn to fidget. She didn't want to think about her altercation with the serial killer. "He's not a psychopath," she finally responded. "He's a monster. There's a difference. If we're going to find Gillian, I had to get something of his. I could sense that pendant was very personal to him. We needed it."

"She'll be proud of you," Slade announced then gently touched her face while staring into her eyes. "I'm proud of you. Especially since you didn't get yourself killed."

Slade pulled her closer. Jolynn placed her hands to his chest and attempted to keep some distance between them, but his arm around her waist kept her close. Jolynn stared at him with a look of concern.

"Slade, what are you doing?"

"I'm going to kiss you," he casually replied. "Any objections?"

Her eyes strayed to his mouth with some hesitation then returned to meet his gaze. She was more frightened of what she'd learn than unwilling.

"You should know even with the heavy painkillers, if you kiss me, you'll completely open your mind," she informed him. "I'll know all your dirty secrets."

"I've been emotionally dead for over a year," he replied with little concern to her admission. "I'm finally feeling something other than hate and revenge. You're welcome to whatever information you can find."

Slade kissed her gently but passionately on the mouth. Jolynn hesitated then returned the kiss while clinging to him. She saw a cluster of images and scenes from his past flashing through her mind. Images of Slade's childhood, his younger sister, their teenage years, his mother's death, and him taking care of his sister. The more passionate their kiss became, the faster the images flashed. An image flashed of Slade's sister and the Pen Pal. In another image, she saw his sister brutally butchered. Jolynn twitched but didn't break off the kiss. His pursuit of the Pen Pal unfolded in her mind, including a scene from their recent hospital visit. Images began to flash of Gillian, the Pen Pal, and herself. She saw the grim reaper. The Pen Pal attacked her. Slade came to rescue her and...

Jolynn suddenly gasped then realized she was lying across the bed with Slade partially on top of her while kissing her throat. Slade abruptly pulled back and looked into her eyes with concern.

"Are you okay?"

Jolynn stared at him with a horrified expression and a strange realization. She knew what she'd seen. She knew what the future had in store for him, and there was nothing she could do to prevent it.

"Is something wrong?"

Jolynn stared at him a moment longer, fighting her tears. She then smiled gently. "No, everything's fine."

Without warning, she placed her arms around his neck, pulled him back down on top of her, and kissed him passionately with startling aggression.   Slade stopped her and offered a warm, concerned smile.

"Remember what the doctor said about hanky but absolutely no panky," he announced gently.

She stared into his eyes through the dim lighting.   All she could see was his impending death at the hands of a psycho killer. She offered a warm smile despite wanting to cry.

"I've been emotionally dead for over *twenty* years," she repeated his earlier comment.   "I'm ready to feel something."

He held back his grin.   "What do doctors know anyway?" Slade remarked then covered her mouth with his and kissed her passionately.

Chapter Thirty-four

Early Monday morning, the sun barely poked through the sheer curtains in Jolynn's bedroom. Slade held Jolynn in his arms and gently stroked her hair while she rested her head on his bare chest. He wore a contented smile although she couldn't see it and lovingly kissed her forehead.

"So--" he gently teased while caressing her shoulder, "do you know all my dirty little secrets?"

She chuckled softly in her throat as she gently ran her fingers through his chest hair. She didn't bother to lift her head. "I'm afraid so, but they're safe with me."

Slade gently caressed her naked back and shoulder. "Do you believe in love at first sight?"

Jolynn was surprised by the question. Well, surprised hearing it come from him. She slowly lifted her head and looked at him with a slightly humored smile.

"Not really," she casually replied.

He chuckled softly while gazing into her eyes. "I didn't want to leave your office the other day. Something about you *captivated* me."

She was surprised to hear him admit he was attracted to her. He had a strange way of showing it. "I thought you were rude and insufferable," she easily admitted.

"I didn't want to be nice to you," he admitted and held her close against him. "I didn't want you being nice to me."

She strained to look at him, but he intentionally held her against his chest, so she couldn't see his expression.

"Why?"

He was reluctant to speak then finally drew a deep breath and continued. "When a man becomes so consumed with anger and revenge, there's seldom room for anything else," Slade informed her. "I haven't even thought about desire in over a year. I've been so consumed with stopping the Pen Pal; it became my life. I wanted to hate the world, so I had to make sure the world hated me just as much."

She considered the comment and managed a soft laugh. "I guess I can understand that," she replied. "In a way, I'm the same. I push people away, because getting to know them even casually becomes far too intimate. One touch and I know half their life. It's a lot to carry."

"I couldn't even imagine the hell you must go through," he announced. "I don't like knowing everything about people I like let alone complete strangers."

They laughed softly and resumed cuddling.

"So now that we've crossed the boundaries into lovers," he finally announced, "will my touch still make you turn and run?"

She laughed softly. "Considering all the contact we've had, I'd say you have nothing left to hide," she informed him then lifted her head to meet his gaze and offered a warm smile. "You're the open book I've completely read."

"Funny--I don't feel violated," he teased then tensed slightly. "I assume you've accepted my past and aren't frightened by what you saw."

"The Pen Pal was your sister's boyfriend?" she gently asked with apprehension. "She was the first victim?"

Slade pulled her into his arms and held her against him in a warm embrace. As he rested his cheek to her head, she could feel him shiver slightly.

"She met him on-line in one of those singles chat rooms. I met him just that once quite by accident," Slade gently informed her. "He wasn't quite the artist he is today, although his mask was more Aztec and less 'horror show' back then. He killed her in the downstairs lounge. I'd arrived just as he was writing with her blood. We struggled, and he took off. The police went looking for him but never found him." He sighed softly. "I tracked down his home through his on-line account. Not so much a home as a satanic torture chamber in a condemned building."

"So you blew it up?"

"Yes, and I enjoyed it very much. Pity he wasn't inside," Slade grumbled with disgust. His look turned softer. "Does it bother you? My idea of the grieving process?"

"No, I wish he had been inside too."

Slade looked past her to the bedside clock. It was five o'clock in the morning. He looked back at her.

"I'm going to take a shower then get us some coffee," Slade announced as he released her.

Jolynn nodded and cuddled the pillow in an attempt to retain some of the warmth. Slade kissed her on the forehead then left the bedroom.

Chapter Thirty-five

Slade's silhouette was clearly visible through the frosted glass door of the phone booth sized standing shower in the bathroom. As the shower ran, steam rose above the glass shower doors, filling the small bathroom. Slade could be heard happily humming while he lathered his body. Just down the hall, within the living room, the apartment doorknob moved slightly then jiggled before turning. The door slowly creaked open then stopped when it hit the chain. Within Jolynn's bedroom, discarded clothing from both sexes was scattered carelessly across the floor. Jolynn wore Slade's shirt while sleeping peacefully beneath the covers. A faint crack was heard deep within the apartment. Jolynn slowly woke with some disorientation and looked around the dimly lit room.

"Slade?"

She could hear the shower still running in the bathroom just down the hall. Jolynn smiled and returned her head to the pillow, nuzzling it. Her eyes again opened as her smile slowly faded into some unfounded preoccupation. The slightly musky male scent from Slade's shirt invaded her senses. Prior to falling asleep, she found the scent pleasing, but now she was overwhelmed by it. She could almost see Slade in the shower. What should have been an erotic fantasy now caused her to shiver at the image as an overwhelming feeling of dread swept over her.

Within the steam-filled bathroom, Slade stood beneath the hot streams of water and allowed it to sooth his strained muscles. He heard someone moving within the hallway just outside the partially open bathroom door. Slade looked toward the frosted glass doors, considered the sound he'd heard, and then smiled lustfully.

"Jo, joining me?"

There was no response. Slade opened the shower door and peered into the cramped bathroom filled with women's personal hygiene products. There was no one there, and he didn't see anyone beyond the slightly open door to the hallway. Slade tapped his fingers on the glass door and sank into thought.

†

There was just enough light from the hallway to partially brighten Jolynn's otherwise dark bedroom. The unsuspecting woman was bundled beneath the covers where she slept peacefully. A shadow appeared in the stream of light from the hallway. The Pen Pal, his face hidden beneath the grotesque mask, quietly stalked with catlike reflexes across the bedroom toward his unsuspecting victim. He clutched his decorative dagger in his gloved hand then hesitated by the bedside. The Pen Pal leaped onto his victim beneath the sheets and plunged the dagger into the mass. He suddenly hesitated, pulled the knife free, and cast back the sheets to reveal pillows beneath him. He appeared stunned by the deception and quickly looked around the room. A muffled gunshot resembling a gust of air exploded the mattress from beneath the bed just inches from him, almost striking him in the shoulder.

The Pen Pal cast himself off the bed, landing on his feet, and dropped to the floor, prepared to strike the hiding woman. Beneath the bed, Jolynn flipped onto her side with Slade's gun in her hand, aimed it at him, and fired again. The bullet grazed his thigh. He leaped to his feet while grasping his bleeding thigh and darted from the room. As the Pen Pal thundered down the hallway, Slade stepped out of the bathroom in his boxer shorts. He was plowed to the floor by the large, fast moving man in the frightening clown zombie mask. Slade slowly moved to his knees and attempted to collect himself while making sense of what had just happened. He then witnessed Jolynn running down the hall past him, wearing only his shirt.

"Come back here, you bastard!"

Slade scrambled to his feet and ran after her. Jolynn charged into the third floor corridor and nearly fell to the floor, failing to negotiate the doorway. The Pen Pal was already near the stairs. Once she regained her balance, Jolynn fired several muffled shots. Had it not been for the silencer on Slade's gun, she would have woken the entire apartment building. The Pen Pal darted down the stairs, narrowly avoiding further injury.

Jolynn thundered down the carpeted hall in her bare feet, making a distinctive thumping sound as she ran. Slade appeared in the apartment doorway with a look of shock on his face at what he'd just witnessed. Despite only wearing a pair of boxer shorts, he ran down the hall after her. Jolynn raced down the stairs with the gun firmly in her hand. She could hear the thundering footfalls of the Pen Pal a level below her and more footfalls on the level above her. She heard the back door on ground level strike the wall harshly as it was thrown open. Jolynn reached the lower door and charged through it without considering he could be on the other side ready to ambush her.

As Jolynn appeared from the back door of the building, she heard the squealing of tires. The same white van rocketed from the parking lot in the dim lighting of few street lamps. It was Deja vu all over again. Slade ran out the back door just behind her. Jolynn clutched her head with the gun still in her hand and screamed as she fell to her knees.

"Oh, God! Gillian," she screamed while sobbing. "I'm so sorry!"

Slade pulled her to her feet and collected her in his arms, holding her against his slightly damp body. He reclaimed his gun from her hand and whisked her inside before she drew anyone's attention.

Chapter Thirty-six

Jolynn sat at the island counter huddled over her cup of coffee while Slade sat alongside her, offering a sympathetic look. It was nearly an hour after their impromptu run-in with the notorious killer. Both were dressed and waiting for response from his team on their patrol of the area. Jolynn was out of sorts and couldn't think straight any longer. Slade continued to watch her with a concerned look.

"We're going to find him, Jolynn," he gently assured her.

"I could have ended this," she replied softly while sniffing. "If only I hadn't missed when I shot at him, he wouldn't have gotten away."

"That's not your fault," he insisted. "That was probably the first time you've ever fired a weapon. No one expects you to be an expert marksman."

She looked at him with fear and concern. "What was he doing here?"

Slade drew a deep breath while staring at her. "I think he came back for his pendant necklace," he informed her. "You were right, it must be important to him."

Jolynn looked back at her cup of coffee and stared, drifting into another world. Slade's phone rang where it rested on the counter near them. He answered it before it finished ringing the first time.

"Slade," he announced into the phone.

"Found something interesting at the coroner's office," Rush announced from the other end.

"Oh?"

"That woman they found dead at the theater," he announced. "The coroner found a picture tucked inside her bra. She'd been stabbed in the chest, but I think the important part of the picture is still intact. I'm sending you a copy."

"Thanks, Rush."

Slade disconnected the call and immediately checked his email. He studied the picture a moment then eyed Jolynn, who was now interested.

"They found a picture hidden on the dead actress's body," Slade informed her. "It must have been important to her. Possibly the reason why she called the deputy earlier that day. Can you get a read on a picture?"

Jolynn sighed with defeat. "Doubtful," she remarked and sulked over her coffee. She straightened and faced Slade. "Couldn't hurt though."

Slade showed her the picture on his camera. The picture was of Loni and Beth, although Jolynn only recognized Beth. A portion of the picture was destroyed by the knife piercing Loni's chest. Jolynn suddenly leaned forward and squinted, staring at the damaged edge of the picture. She stared a moment longer and recognized what little image was left of the man in the background. Her eyes suddenly widened and her hand covered her mouth with horror.

"That's Dan!"

"What? Who?" Slade asked and eyed the picture.

"In the background," she gasped and pointed at the picture on the cell phone. "It's hard to tell, but it's Dan, I know it."

"Okay," Slade replied. "So this guy Dan is in the background of the picture. Is that important?"

"Considering he's a notorious ladies' man, it might be," Jolynn announced with enthusiasm. "She hid it on her body for some reason. Maybe she remembered something involving him."

"So we should talk to this Dan," Slade replied. "Where do we find him?"

"He works at the hospital with me."

"I wonder why the coroner hadn't made the same connection?" Slade remarked in curious observation.

"With two gorgeous women in the frame, I doubt he even noticed some random guy in the background," Jolynn informed him. "Besides, it's not like he's friends with Dan. Most men aren't." She sprang up from her chair. "I need to touch him. We don't have a moment to lose. If he's involved, we need to know right away."

"It's Monday," Slade announced and stood as well. "Will he be at the hospital today?"

"He should already be there," she replied. "I called off earlier this morning, but it wouldn't look suspicious if I showed up to explain to Mr. McQueen why I called out."

"Then we'll go to the hospital and pay this Dan a visit," Slade replied then gave her a strange look. "But don't you think if Dan was a serial killer you'd have sensed something long ago?"

"No," she replied. "I avoid touching people, and if I never had something personal of theirs, I doubt I'd ever know. I don't have any personal connections to anyone I work with. That's by design."

"Okay then," Slade replied. "We'll leave as soon as you're ready."

"I'm ready."

✝

Slade and Jolynn entered the medical records room and looked around. Rush sat behind Jolynn's desk with his feet propped on top and played games on his cell phone. He looked up when they entered and immediately planted his feet on the floor.

"That was fast," Rush announced while replacing his cell phone to his inner jacket pocket. "That Deputy Hunt guy is still informally questioning your boy."

Both eyed Rush suspiciously.

"Deputy Hunt?" Slade asked. "You called the police before we had a chance to talk to Dan?"

"No, don't be stupid," Rush snapped and glared at Slade through narrow eyes. "You think your girl there is the only one who noticed the kid in the background? Some nurse showed up. Friends with the coroner, I guess. He showed her the picture, and she pointed him out." He snorted a soft laugh. "Wasn't exactly fond of him either. Apparently, he gets around *and* he'd been friendly with the first murdered woman."

Slade glanced at Jolynn with question in his eyes. "No chance he's aware of your psychic abilities, is there? We don't want him turning into a flight risk now that the police are questioning him."

"Trust me," Jolynn announced dryly. "I haven't told anyone; not even Gillian. The last time I said anything to anyone was when I was eight. I told my parents, and they sent me to a psychiatrist. I've never told anyone since. Well, except you."

"That's a relief," Slade replied with a relaxed sigh.

The door opened and McQueen entered. He saw Jolynn and the two men and immediately stopped just inside the room with a surprised look. He eyed both men then looked back at Jolynn.

"I thought you called in today," McQueen announced with a strange look on his face.

"I did," she replied, "but I thought I should let you know what happened."

"That's not necessary," McQueen announced while waving her off. "When do you ever call in sick? If you say you're sick, I believe you." He again eyed both men and offered a moderately polite nod to Slade. "Agent Slade. I didn't think you'd be back again so soon. What do I owe the pleasure?"

"We're here to talk to one of the hospital employees," Slade informed him.

"Dan?" McQueen suddenly asked and appeared curious. "What's going on around here? Is he in some sort of trouble?" Without waiting for a response, he looked back at Jolynn and cocked his head to the side. "Is it true, Jolynn? Are you some sort of psychic?"

There was an odd silence across the room as they exchanged looks. Jolynn fidgeted and looked at her boss.

"Who told you that?" she asked while insecurely holding her elbows.

"Are you kidding? It's all over the hospital," McQueen announced while giving her a strange look. It was a look she'd seen many times before. She hated that look. "Deputy Hunt told Sam you were working with the FBI. I guess Sam told everyone else. Coroner's love to gossip." He continued to stare at her. "Why didn't you say anything?"

"I don't like to talk about it," she replied softly and continued to fidget. "It's like living with a curse."

"Are you kidding?" McQueen announced while grinning. "I think that's awesome! Are you going to pull some psychic shit on Dan? Is that why you're here to see him?"

Slade and Rush exchanged looks. Both men groaned.

"I'll keep an eye on the kid, so he doesn't make the great escape after the deputy is finished with him," Rush announced and hurried from the room.

McQueen watched Rush leave, appeared concerned, and looked at Slade. "Did I say something wrong?"

"No," Slade announced with a dreary sigh. "That would be Deputy Hunt's faux pas."

McQueen looked back at Jolynn and grinned. "So tell me about this talent of yours," he announced cheerfully. "What sort of cool things can you do?" His look suddenly turned serious. "You can't move things with your mind, can you?"

Jolynn groaned softly and eyed Slade. He offered a reassuring smile along with a tiny shrug. Rush hurried into the office with a hostile look on his face.

"Our little chicken flew the coup," he announced with annoyance. "Apparently, he heard about your girl's psychic abilities and panicked. Sounds like a guilty man to me."

Slade cursed softly under his breath. "Didn't Deputy Hunt think to keep an eye on him until we got here?"

"No, I suppose he didn't," Rush snarled. "He's out looking for him now."

"Onto plan 'B'," Slade announced with a soft groan.

Chapter Thirty-seven

The police car pulled up to the old, two-story house just on the outskirts of town only a few minutes' drive from the hospital. It was already early afternoon and no one had been able to find Dan after he took off from the hospital. There were very few homes located around Dan's family home but most appeared abandoned. The nearby area was being developed and most of the homes were sold to the developers. Deputy Hunt sat behind the wheel of his police cruiser and stared at the old house on the poorly tended lot. The weeds were overgrown and excess trash had been strewn along the sides of the road. He lacked confidence as he stared at the creepy, abandoned house. Hunt pressed a button on his cell phone and placed it to his ear.

"Hey, Thelma," he announced into the phone. "Are you sure this is the address? The place looks condemned."

"That's the suspect's mother's last known address," the woman on the other end responded.

He groaned softly, obviously not thrilled with the prospect of going anywhere near the house. "I'm going to check it out," Hunt announced in a slightly squeaky voice. "Call me if the other deputies have any luck at his apartment in town."

"You want backup, Hunt?" Thelma asked over the phone.

He again eyed the building, drew a deep, shaken breath, and put on a brave front. "No, there's nothing to indicate anyone's been here in months or even years," Hunt replied. "I'm going to check it out quick just to be sure."

Hunt disconnected the call, placed the phone in his pocket, and got out of the police cruiser. He cautiously approached the house while keeping his hand nervously on his nightstick. Nothing around the yard indicated anyone had been through the yard let alone within the house. He stepped onto the porch, which creaked loudly beneath his feet causing him to tense slightly. He exhaled and approached the door. Deputy Hunt knocked on the door then peered in through the dirty, single pane glass. The home didn't contain any furniture and the place was covered in cobwebs. A thick layer of dust on the floor revealed no footprints. Deputy Hunt shook his head and left the porch. He walked around the house and peered into several windows, but nothing indicated anyone had been in or near the house in a long time. The only bent blades of grass were the ones he'd left behind.

After checking all the doors and windows, the conclusion was the same. No one had entered the house. He headed back to his police car while scanning the rest of the dilapidated neighborhood. Hunt approached his cruiser and jumped inside with a soft groan. He removed his phone and pressed the same button.

"Hey, Thelma," he announced into the phone with a little more confidence. "The house is abandoned. I'm on my way back to the hospital. Maybe he's hanging out around there."

"Okay, Hunt," she replied from the other end.

He disconnected the call and stared out the windshield of the cruiser a moment before putting the car into gear. As Hunt looked behind him to back up, he caught a glimpse of something within the backseat. He gasped while whirling his head around to look in the seat behind him. The tip of a decorative dagger pierced through his left eye and easily passed through into his brain, stopping when it scraped bone at the back of the skull. Deputy Hunt's body jerked and jolted as the dagger was pulled free along with a gusher of blood. His body violently collapsed against the driver's seat while blood ran from his pierced eye socket. The back door of the cruiser closed, and the faint sound of cheerful whistling was heard trialing off.

†

Later that afternoon, Jolynn and Slade sat with his men at the kitchen table in Jolynn's apartment. All six were huddled over cups of coffee. Slade had a map of the county spread across the kitchen table with all eleven victims from the entire year boldly marked in red. The five men studied the map closely as if anticipating the answer to some unknown riddle. The rules had changed and their lives were now on the line the same as Gillian. The Pen Pal knew who they were and where to find them. They had little choice but to find him first.

Jolynn sat on a kitchen chair, hugging her knees to her chest while staring fixated on the silver pendant attached to the black, leather cord within her hands. With the leather cord in each hand, she rotated the pendant frontward then backward. Slade glanced at Jolynn several times and appeared distracted by her sedate behavior. She'd been in another world since the killer broke into her apartment and then got away. She blamed herself for not killing him when she had the chance. Slade looked back at the map and attempted to concentrate.

"Here's the house where you found Gillian's credit card," Slade informed his men. "We spooked him enough to relocate her. He doesn't have much time, so he won't go far." He looked at his men and stiffened. "We need to locate every private, abandoned place on or around the outskirts of town."

All four men shifted in their chairs and offered groans of defeat.

"That's a long shot, Slade," Wilson boldly remarked, being the only one to speak what the others were thinking.

Slade vigorously ran his fingers through his hair while leaning back in his chair. "I know, but we have no choice," he announced and sighed. "Anything on that tooth fragment you found at the warehouse?"

"Yeah," Wilson replied. "Turns out it's acrylic resin. It's very popular for dentures."

"Our killer wears dentures?" Carl asked with a look of surprise.

"When he came after me, I saw his teeth were filed to points, like his mouth was filled with canine teeth," Slade informed them. "Maybe they were actually canine dentures. He could have broken one during the attack."

"But that doesn't get us anywhere," Baxter snarled with limited patience.

Jolynn continued to play with the twirling pendant and barely acknowledged the conversation. Baxter glanced at Jolynn then looked back at Slade.

"What's wrong with her?" Baxter asked.

"Shock, I think," he replied then looked at the distracted woman. "Jolynn--?"

She didn't respond. Wilson appeared equally concerned and watched her.

"I don't know what to do," Slade remarked with defeat. "Time's running out for Gillian. In this state, she won't be able to help us."

"Then we need to leave her and get back to finding this guy," Baxter informed him firmly. "That's what we're being paid to do."

"Oh, real sensitive, Baxter," Wilson snarled.

"I'm not being paid to be sensitive," Baxter lashed back. "Can we get back to our mission?"

Slade nodded and shifted with a certain uneasiness. "I'm sorry," he replied. "I'm having a tough time focusing. Where were we?"

"Wasting time," Baxter snapped.

"Knock it off, Baxter," Rush growled.

Slade once more looked back at Jolynn. She continued to play with the Pen Pal's pendant, allowing it to rotate forward and backward like a spinning wheel. Her eyes narrowed as she stared at the rotating symbol. It rotated faster.

"Jolynn, stop playing," Slade scolded. "We need you to look at the map."

She didn't respond. All eyes were now on Jolynn and the pendant that rotated faster and faster. Her actions were more than a mere distraction now. She stared intently at the pendant.

"What's she--?" Wilson began.

Slade held his hand up and silenced him. Jolynn continued to stare at the center of the pendant. She saw flashes of an old house set in the country with a dark cloud looming over it. Lightning struck violently.

"Yep, she's gone," Carl muttered.

Jolynn suddenly stopped the pendant. Silence surrounded the table as they all stared, uncertain what to make of her actions. Jolynn took the pendant and slammed it down on the map in the center of the red dots. She pointed to the hole on the far left of the pendant over the map.

"He's there."

They uncertainly looked at the map.

Slade looked back at Jolynn as his brows knitted. "Are you sure?" he questioned. "That's not his typical pattern. That's on the opposite side of River Run. Why would he go there?"

Jolynn stood, snatched the red marker, and began to draw lines along the symbol onto the map. Each point touched a red dot. She pulled the pendant back allowing them to see the symbol was now drawn on the map. The only point missing was to the far left of the symbol.

Slade looked at his men and stood. "You heard the lady," he announced with conviction. "That's where we're going."

They quickly gathered their maps and their coffee and hurried from the kitchen. Jolynn was about to follow when Slade stopped her. She looked at him with the same glazed expression she'd had since that morning.

"Are you okay?"

"No, not really," Jolynn replied in a mildly sedate tone. "Promise me you'll get her back alive. Promise he won't do to her what he did to those other women."

"I promise I'll do everything I can," Slade insisted while caressing her shoulders. "I need your help though. I'm counting on you to get us there."

"I'll get you there. Don't worry about me," she insisted. "The place he's taken Gillian must be personal to him. That's why it's not his typical pattern."

"That also means he's going to be on the defensive more than he already is," Slade remarked. "There's no telling what we're going to be walking into."

"You must realize he's completely insane. Getting into his mind is pretty frightening, but I can always find my way back to reality." She played with the pendant while studying it. "As long as I hold this, I'm linked to him."

"Then you'd better hang onto it," Slade informed her while holding back his concern. "There isn't much time left, and we need all the help we can get."

Chapter Thirty-eight

Slade's replacement rental car and the black van drove along the abandoned back road far from any homes or businesses. They drove through vast nothingness in the early evening, which was even indicated as nothing on the map. Slade drove a little slower while Jolynn clutched the pendant and kept her eyes closed. She'd been silent over an hour, which wasn't helping Slade's anxiety. Slade glanced at her several times with a look of worry to where they were heading, since there was nothing before them, and the sun was already beginning to set.

"Can you get us there, Jolynn?" he finally asked, breaking the silence.

She seemed to be off in her own world, and she hadn't responded to several earlier questions. It was becoming concerning. Slade shifted behind the wheel and attempted to remain calm.

Her eyes suddenly popped open. "Stop."

Slade stopped the car, nearly squealing the tires. He looked around with some apprehension. All they saw were fields, woods, and rolling hills. The van sharply stopped behind Slade's car, coming close to hitting its rear bumper. There was nothing but farmland and sporadic trees. Slade looked around the rapidly diming area amidst the setting sun.

"We're in the middle of a field," he delicately informed her, his impatience starting to show.

Jolynn looked out her side window and gently indicated the overgrown field. "There's an old, private lane to the right."

He strained to look beyond the field on her side then shook his head. "There's nothing there," Slade firmly insisted. "It's a field."

"Turn," she ordered. "Turn right here."

Slade sighed and turned off the rarely used back road into the overgrown field with two faint marks of tire tracks grown over from years past. Areas of the thick brush had been recently trampled, which was somewhat encouraging. Within the van, Carl sat behind the wheel and watched with surprise as the car before him drove into the field.

"Where the hell is he going?" Carl demanded. "To take a piss?"

The van followed Slade's car along the overgrown path. Just over the small hill, there was the large abandoned farmhouse in severe disrepair. Every window had been boarded, the paint had pealed completely off the siding, and boards on the porch were rotted to the point of being missing. Slade turned off his headlights. The van followed their lead. They drove a little closer then pulled into a dark area alongside a row of trees. As they made their way out of their vehicles, Jolynn stared at the house in the near distance. She felt her entire body involuntarily freeze. All five men attached their cell phones to their belts and inserted their earpieces.

Carl handed out shoulder holsters with semiautomatics and extra magazines. Slade took one for himself and extended one to Jolynn. Jolynn continued to stare at the house without moving or looking away. She watched blood seemingly run down the exterior walls from gashes in the siding that now resembled flesh. She then saw the grim reaper standing on the rotted porch in front of the door. She held her breath and closed her eyes. As she opened her eyes, she saw it was just the old farmhouse. Jolynn continued to stare off at the farmhouse as Slade studied her with the shoulder holster still extended.

"Jolynn, take the gun," he firmly insisted.

Jolynn slowly looked at him then the gun in the holster. She looked back at the house and resumed staring hypnotically. "It's not going to help."

Slade slipped her arm through the shoulder holster and secured it over her other shoulder, tightening it to fit her. He stood directly in front of her to block her view of the farmhouse, forcing her to focus her attention on him.

"Anything you'd like to share with us before we go in there?" he asked.

She stared helplessly into his eyes. "There's death all around that house," Jolynn informed them in a strange, defeated tone. "He's trying to raise the dead--some demon. It's his mentor back from the grave."

All five men exchanged looks. Whether they believed her or not, her words chilled them.

Rush leaned closer to Slade and muttered, "Jolynn's gone bye-bye."

Slade pulled Jolynn aside, turned her to face him, and gently touched her face. Her expression was completely blank, and it was hard to tell if she was actually seeing him or if she was lost in another world.

"Maybe you should wait in the van," he suggested.

She looked back at the house then pulled away from Slade and headed for the porch. Slade groaned while looking at his men.

"You three take the back," Slade announced to Wilson, Baxter, and Rush. "Carl, Jolynn, and I will go through the front entrance."

They nodded and immediately sprang into action. Wilson, Rush, and Baxter ran along the tree line toward the house and around back.

Chapter Thirty-nine

Carl and Slade hurried after Jolynn as she headed toward the farmhouse but the two men remained in the tree line just out of sight. Even if the killer saw her approaching, he wouldn't be frightened off by her. He'd undoubtedly enjoy the thrill of an additional kill. Jolynn didn't seem to notice or care that neither man had been behind her. She had her sights focused on the house and finding her friend.

"What's wrong with her?" Carl asked.

"She's in her own world. I know it doesn't sound rational, but I honestly believe she knows what she's doing," Slade replied then gave his friend a serious look. "That being said; don't let anything happen to her."

Carl cocked his gun and gave a firm, reassuring nod. "You've got it."

Jolynn walked onto the rickety porch as Carl and Slade hurried across the field and joined her. Carl and Slade positioned themselves alongside the door, prepared to break it down, which wouldn't take much effort for the condition it was in. Jolynn stood before the seven-foot tall grim reaper that only she could see. His tattered, black cloak flapped in a breeze that mysteriously didn't touch her. Jolynn stared into the darkness of the hood and tilted her head slightly as if curious. The grim reaper tilted his head in response and appeared to study her as well. She didn't understand why she wasn't afraid of something that should cause fear in most. Slade watched Jolynn as she seemed to stare blankly, from his prospective, at nothing.

"Jolynn, talk to me."

Jolynn continued to stare at the grim reaper standing before her. Her expression was fixated on the figure that stared back. Maybe he was just as curious that she could see him as she was to see him.

"Have you ever stared death in the face?" she whispered to no one in particular.

Slade and Carl exchanged skeptical looks. Slade groaned softly. Carl shook his head then kicked open the door and entered with his gun drawn. Slade pulled Jolynn behind him into the house. The entire house appeared to be filled with candles throughout the firetrap. The old hallway was dilapidated and the plaster appeared to break away from the walls. The candlelight revealed the bloody writing on the walls. Every wall contained the creepy encrypted writing. Carl looked around the walls as Slade and Jolynn entered behind him.

"Yep," Carl announced while nodding. "This is the right place."

Jolynn looked around, gasped with horror, and threw herself against the wall near the door. Everything was hitting her at once, and the overload was almost unbearable. Slade was alarmed by her reaction. It seemed overboard considering everything she had seen in recent days.

"Would you like to wait in the car?" he asked gently.

Jolynn twitched as images flashed in shock waves all at once. She saw brutal scenes of the Pen Pal's murders, blood, and snarling beasts all while listening to horrified screams in her head that would not silence. Jolynn gasped and clutched her head as the nightmares continued to play out before her closed eyes. She saw Gillian lying naked tied on an old table surrounded by candles. She could hear the Pen Pal chanting, but it abruptly stopped. Their assault on the house interrupted his ritual, which was to Gillian's advantage. She could see Gillian fighting the ropes binding her to the table. She was witnessing a vision in present time as she had when her friend was abducted and when Beth was killed. Jolynn saw another image but this one was the future. In her vision, she saw the killer attacking Slade. She watched helplessly as the Pen Pal tore into Slade's throat with his sharp teeth. Jolynn suddenly threw her arms around Slade's neck and clung to him. He held her against him and motioned for Carl to look around. Carl eyed them with uncertainty then moved along the hallway. Jolynn buried her face into Slade's neck, becoming hysterical.

"You can't go," she gasped with concern. "He's going to kill you!"

Slade gently rocked her while holding her head to his chest. "It was me you saw, wasn't it?" he asked. "I'm the tragic lover who dies at the hands of the monster."

Jolynn slowly pulled away, met his gaze as tears ran down her cheeks, and uncertainly nodded. He gently wiped the tears away while staring into her eyes.

"Maybe you foresaw my death, but he's not going to kill me," Slade informed her with conviction. "I'm not ready to die just yet."

"You won't have a choice," she informed him and continued to stare. "Leave."

He was surprised by her comment. "What happened to fate and destiny?" Slade insisted. "What about Gillian?"

"I'll find Gillian," Jolynn informed him. "You need to leave this house."

"I'm coming back for you, Jolynn," Slade reassured her. "But for now, I need to fulfill my own destiny."

Slade kissed her warmly but passionately then pushed her out the open door and onto the porch. He slammed and braced the door shut behind her. Jolynn stood on the porch, momentarily stunned, and then attempted to open the door. It was surprisingly solid. She kicked and pounded on it.

"Slade! No!"

She allowed her head to fall against the door while holding back her tears. A shadow fell over her. Jolynn sniffed and looked alongside her. To her surprise, the reaper stood beside her. She could feel his stare cutting through her.

"You can't have him," Jolynn whispered. "I'm not going to let you take him."

The reaper lowered his sling blade toward the side of the house as if directing her. Jolynn uncertainly looked in the direction the reaper pointed. She looked back at the cloaked figure, slightly skeptical, and then turned and headed off the porch. She hurried around the house toward the back where she saw a shed beyond a large, old tree. Jolynn looked around then ran to the back kitchen door. She attempted to open the door, but it didn't budge. She cried out with frustration while violently kicking it. The reaper again stood alongside her and pointed beyond the kitchen door. Jolynn gave him a puzzled look then observed the old cellar entrance that was barely visible.

"I must be insane," she muttered softly. "Who in their right mind would trust the grim reaper?"

He again pointed with his sling blade, obviously not offended by the comment. He was guiding her. For whatever reason, he intended to help her get inside. Was he attempting to fulfill a fate that involved her death, or was he actually helping her? It didn't matter at the moment. Jolynn ran for the old wooden basement door beyond overgrown shrubs. She pulled on the old latch. The door easily opened, although loudly creaking on rusted hinges. She hesitated to the sight of blood trailing down the old, stone steps. Jolynn cautiously walked down the crumbling steps.

An old door, which was opened inward, led her into the empty fruit cellar. She removed the semiautomatic from the shoulder holster and walked across the enclosed fruit cellar toward the connecting door. She paused a moment and looked at the cobweb covered wall. An old machete with little to no rust hung there. Jolynn snatched the machete from the wall and continued toward the next door. She paused within the large furnace room and looked at the rickety steps leading upstairs. Her body subconsciously trembled. Jolynn drew a determined breath, straightened, and headed up the stairs without further hesitation.

Chapter Forty

Slade led Carl along the back hallway on the first floor. Movement was heard from a nearby room. Slade gave the signal to stop. Both men stood in the hallway and listened but the sound was gone. With their guns in their hands, both men stepped into the kitchen. There was no one there. They looked around and noticed the basement door remained partially open. Slade nodded to Carl. They headed for the basement door. Slade led the way down the rickety basement steps with Carl bringing up the rear. The steps curved with the wall on a small landing before the bottom, leaving a blind spot as to what was ahead. Slade cautiously moved onto the landing, saw nothing, and continued down into the furnace area of the basement. He scanned the area, paying particular attention to dark corners. Carl reached the bottom of the steps and stood behind Slade with his gun drawn and prepared to fire. When nothing moved, they continued past the firewood storage stall, which still contained old wood from decades past.

Something moved in the dark area from behind the steps. As Carl looked back to check it out, the Pen Pal was standing directly behind him. His horrifying mask was enough to stop Carl in his tracks. Before Carl could react or even gasp, the killer's decorative dagger was thrust downward into Carl's throat, keeping him from screaming. Slade turned to the sound of parting air and the gruesome sound as the knife sliced into Carl's flesh. All he witnessed was Carl falling to the floor and a shadow running up the steps just out of sight. Slade leaped to Carl's side, kneeling alongside him. Carl gasped twice as the blood flowed rapidly from his throat. He stopped mid gasp, having taken his last breath, and stared blankly. Slade cursed softly then slowly straightened while keeping his eyes on the stairs. He grabbed Carl's gun, stuck it down the back of his pants, and hurried up the stairs after the killer.

✝

Jolynn walked cautiously and quietly along the first floor hallway. Something compelled her to stop before the sliding, wooden doors to the dining room. She stared at the closed door a moment then slowly pulled the sliding door open. She stood in the doorway with the gun in her right hand and the machete in her left. There were dozens of candles lining the dining room and more bloody writing on the walls. Gillian lay naked and bound on the dining room table. Added ropes held her midsection immobile against the table as well to prevent her from wiggling loose. She fought against her ropes and duct tape covering her mouth, unable to see who had entered, but she obviously heard someone opening the door. Jolynn wasn't sure if she was relieved or frightened to death as she rushed across the room to Gillian's side. Gillian muffled a scream to the presence of someone near her then finally got a look at her friend standing over her. Shock flooded Gillian's frightened face.

"It's okay, Gillian," Jolynn announced in rushed whisper. "I'm here."

Jolynn removed the duct tape from her mouth, allowing her friend to gasp with relief. After her ordeal, a friendly face must have been a great comfort. The astonished look on Gillian's face having seen her friend standing over her told a complex story.

"Oh, Jolynn. I can't believe you're actually here," Gillian gasped in a frantic but hushed tone, the tears swelling in her eyes. She fought her emotions to keep from breaking down. After all she'd been through; Gillian had every right to break down. Although now wasn't that time and both women knew it. "Thank God! Get me out of here before he comes back!"

"I'll have you out in a minute," Jolynn whispered back, holding off on the tearful reunion herself.

Jolynn took a moment to assess the thick ropes and their complex knots. Rather than work on the complex knots holding her friend captive, Jolynn raised the machete and hacked the rope binding her wrists to the table. It took a few thrusts, being the machete was slightly dull, but the ropes finally snapped and fell from her friend's naked body. Gillian half sat up while trembling with fear and exhaustion. Jolynn rounded the table and cut through the ropes binding her ankles. Gillian attempted to stand on her own, unwilling to wait for assistance, and nearly fell from the table. Jolynn caught her friend to keep her from hitting the floor. Gillian clung to her in a tight embrace and nearly sobbed.

The rush of images from her friend's entire life aside, Jolynn knew they didn't have time for a joyful reunion. She pulled away and scanned the room, spotting Gillian's clothes lying nearby on the floor. Jolynn hurriedly grabbed her friend's discarded clothing and helped her dress while keeping watch on both the closed kitchen door and the open hallway door. Despite how many people were roaming around the large house, it was surprisingly quiet. The near silence made Jolynn uneasy. Gillian trembled while quickly slipping into her clothing, fumbling with each article.

"The man who took me," Gillian whispered in rushed speech, "he's psychotic." She clung to Jolynn's arm once she'd finished dressing. The fear in Gillian's eyes was beyond description. "He won't hesitate to kill us both. Please tell me you brought the police."

"Considering our theory on where to find you, the police never would have believed us," Jolynn replied softly then handed her friend the machete while she clutched the gun. "We have backup though. They've been hunting this guy a long time. They'll take care of him. It's my job to get you out of here." She looked at her friend and held her breath. "Are you ready?"

Gillian clutched the machete in sweaty palms then exhaled softly and nodded with conviction.

Chapter Forty-one

Slade entered the second floor hallway from the back kitchen stairs and scanned the area with his gun aimed. The hallway was quiet and only dimly lit by a few stray candles. Every bedroom door along the second floor hallway was left open, leaving vast darkness beyond each door. The killer could be hiding in any of the rooms just waiting for someone to walk past. Slade placed a finger to his ear transmitter while keeping his back to the wall at the top of the stairs.

"Anyone see him?" Slade asked softly, keeping careful watch of the hallway and the stairs to his left.

"Negative," came the responses over the transmitter from his remaining men.

"He headed upstairs," Slade informed them. "I'm on the second floor now."

"Want backup, Slade?" Wilson asked through Slade's ear transmitter.

"No, this house is a virtual maze," Slade remarked while appearing uneasy. "If he made it to the front stairs already, he could be anywhere. Stay alert."

Slade cautiously walked along the second floor hall, keeping his back to the wall as he approached one of the bedrooms. There was a faint glow from within the first bedroom. Slade paused near the open doorway. He removed his flashlight and kept it steady beneath his gun. As he turned on the flashlight, he leaped into the doorway, casting his back to the frame, and aimed his gun into the room. He swept the room with his flashlight, keeping the gun aimed above the light. Nothing within the room moved. He shined his light toward the corner and the dim glow from three small candles where several mattresses were piled on the floor.

A young woman wearing a white, satin nightgown and a white lacy scarf around her neck lay on top of the mattresses. It was possible the woman was dead, although there wasn't any blood. Slade again scanned the room with his flashlight before slowly approaching the dead woman. He stopped only a few feet away once he was able to get a better look at her. Slade's expression suddenly dropped as he stared with horror at his dead sister. He lowered his gun and uncertainly approached the motionless woman.

"Angie?" Slade gasped with disbelief.

Slade stopped before the elevated mattresses, unable to take his eyes off her. He fell to his knees, allowing his head to fall to the mattress near the dead woman and sobbed softly over her.

"Oh, Angie," he gasped in anguish. "I'm so sorry. If only I'd gotten to you sooner. I should have killed him when I had the chance."

A shadow loomed in the doorway behind him, but he was so consumed with grief, he didn't notice. Slade finally sniffed while slowly lifting his head and wiped his tears to his sleeve in the hand with his gun. The Pen Pal slowly approached Slade from behind while raising his decorative dagger. Slade again wiped his eyes and looked at the dead woman. To his shock and horror, it wasn't his sister. He saw the severely decayed woman with rats crawling over her partially chewed body. Slade gasped with horror and straightened on his knees.

One of the candles flickered. Slade whirled around still on his knees. The Pen Pal thrust down with the dagger. Slade cried out while casting himself from the path of the knife. The knife struck the mattress, fully embedded near the dead woman. He quickly pulled the knife free and turned toward Slade. Slade aimed his gun at the same time from where he half sat on the floor. The Pen Pal kicked Slade in the face, knocking him onto his backside and tossing the gun across the room.

"He's here!" Slade shouted into his transmitter. "Wilson! I need backup!"

The Pen Pal lunged for Slade with the dagger prepared to strike. The sound of heavy footfalls thundered in the hallway not far from the room. The Pen Pal was taken by surprise at the sound. He straightened and disappeared into a dark corner of the room. Slade scrambled to his feet, grabbing his discarded gun and flashlight. He scanned the room with the flashlight, prepared to shoot the first thing that moved. He wasn't there! Rush and Wilson appeared in the bedroom doorway with their own weapons aimed and shined their lights on Slade.

"Where'd he go?" Rush asked.

Slade lowered his gun and shook his head. "He was right here," he protested. "I didn't see him leave the room." Slade sprang to his feet. "He has to be in here."

All three shined their flashlights around the empty room. Rush shined his light into the empty closet, which stood open. They exchanged puzzled looks.

"There's something messed up with this house," Wilson announced. "He couldn't have just vanished. He's not some goddamned demon."

"Could there be secret passageways?" Rush questioned with concern.

"It's the only logical answer," Slade replied with disgust while looking around. "You guys take the main stairs. I'll take the back stairs."

All three hurried from the bedroom. Slade headed for the back kitchen stairs while his men headed for the front stairs, carefully peering into each dark room as they passed.

Slade tapped his ear transmitter. "Baxter, continue your search for the girl."

"Affirmative," Baxter responded. "There's some fresh kill down here, though I don't think it's our girl."

Slade cautiously peered into the narrow stairway, keeping his flashlight trained on the dark, narrow steps. "Copy. Proceed with caution."

†

Wilson and Rush appeared at the bottom of the main staircase with their guns drawn. Both looked around the candlelit hallway then exchanged looks. Wilson nodded Rush to the right then he went left. Rush cautiously approached the right side of the hall and entered the first room. Wilson headed to the left and down the hall, pausing outside the open living room doorway. He leaped into the doorway with his gun aimed and looked around the candlelit living room. Some old, cobweb infested furniture and tattered curtains covering the large windows were all that remained within the creepy room. Wilson slowly entered the living room and looked around with his gun guiding the way. The glow of several strategically placed candles created many dark corners and cast dancing shadows on the walls. The old, tattered curtain moved away from the large window.

Wilson approached the curtain with some apprehension. Since all the windows were boarded, there shouldn't have been any airflow to move the dusty curtains. He hesitated a foot from the curtains then pulled them back. There was a hole in the glass and a broken board just outside, allowing for wind flow. Wilson groaned softly and released the curtain, allowing it to fall back in place. He turned and came face-to-face with the creepy zombie clown mask of the Pen Pal. The Pen Pal knocked the gun from his hand, tossing it across the room, and attempted to stab Wilson with his bloodied dagger. Wilson cried out and caught his wrist, keeping the knife from piercing him.

"Rush!" Wilson cried out.

"On my way," Rush replied through his ear transmitter, although his voice was also heard in the hallway, indicating he was close by.

With his free hand, Wilson punched the Pen Pal in the stomach. Although it didn't even faze him, he appeared annoyed by the effort.

"Wilson, what's your location?" Slade could be heard through his ear transmitter.

Wilson was about to respond when the Pen Pal grabbed him by the throat and lifted him in the air, pulling him off his feet. Wilson gasped beneath the hand crushing his throat but was unable to respond to the men with his location. Rush appeared in the doorway and aimed his gun.

"I have him, Slade," Rush announced through his ear transmitter while attempting to get a clean shot at the man holding Wilson. "I don't have a clean shot!"

The Pen Pal saw Rush in the doorway and slung Wilson across the room, casting him into his teammate with excessive force. Both men flew from the living room and across the hall floor, striking the opposing wall with a loud thump. The frail wall immediately cracked, creating dirt and dust powdering across the fallen men. Both men coughed and attempted to gain their bearings. They looked around, but there was no sign of the stealthy killer.

Chapter Forty-two

Jolynn led Gillian into the old, outdated kitchen, although considered quite modern back when the house was first built. A fire was burning in the pit used for cooking, giving enough of a glow to brighten most of the kitchen area. As they headed for the outer kitchen door, they head a strange, loud clunk possibly radiating from the basement beneath the kitchen. Whatever the sound, it echoed throughout the room as if coming at them from all sides. Both looked around with concern and some confusion. Gillian clutched Jolynn's hand and practically pulled her toward the outside door. She grabbed the doorknob and pulled on the door, but it wouldn't open. She tried the lock, but it became clearly evident that the lock wasn't the issue. Jolynn looked around while deep in thought.

"That sound," Jolynn softly informed her friend. "It sounded like metal scraping metal." She looked back at the kitchen door and studied it. "We're locked in. He activated some sort of locking mechanism on the doors and windows." She looked at Gillian with concern. "That's the sound we heard."

Gillian stared at her friend with alarm. "No, no, no," she gasped with fright and horror. "We've got to get out of here.

We'll try another door. Smash the windows if we have to, but we're getting out of here." She vigorously shook her head. "You don't want to run into this guy, Jolynn. You have no idea what sort of monster he is."

"I think I might," Jolynn replied and looked around. She indicated a nearby door oddly placed to the side of the kitchen. It was possibly a pantry. "Let's see where that door goes."

They hurried across the well-lit kitchen for the side door. Jolynn attempted to open it, but it wouldn't budge. Jolynn snatched the machete from her friend and violently hacked the doorknob. The knob broke loose and rolled across the floor. She easily kicked open the door then returned the machete to Gillian. Gillian stared at the machete a moment then looked back at her friend with some surprise.

"I don't know when you acquired an aggressive streak, but I think I like it," Gillian announced.

Jolynn grabbed her wrist and pulled her friend into the next room while keeping her gun in her free hand. They uncertainly entered the brightly lit room with an excessive number of candles. None of the Pen Pal's victims had been displayed with such passion. That could mean only one thing. Both scanned the room then gasped softly at the sight of the open casket proudly placed on display. Jolynn released Gillian's hand and slowly approached the casket. Gillian sheepishly followed at arm's distance.

"Bad idea," Gillian mumbled softly while scanning the room in fear of someone jumping out at them. "When trapped in a haunted house, you never approach dead guys in caskets."

As Jolynn got closer, she saw the decaying remains of an embalmed man wearing an expensive suit now aged and tattered. Although well preserved, severe decay was still evident.

"Jolynn," Gillian whispered with a quiver in her voice. "I don't like this. Let's get out of here."

Jolynn barely heard her friend as she stared at the neatly dressed corpse and considered his reason for being there. This man obviously meant something to the Pen Pal. He was undeniably someone very important. That left Jolynn with only one choice. She held her breath, pushed aside her fear, and reached into the casket. Gillian held back her gasp by placing her hand to her mouth.

"What the hell are you doing?" she softly cried out with horror. "Don't touch it!"

Jolynn placed her hand on the shriveled, ash colored hand positioned over the dead man's abdomen.

"Come on," Gillian whimpered while tugging on Jolynn's shirt, practically pleading with her friend.

A sudden shockwave struck Jolynn, nearly stealing her breath. Frightening images flooded her mind. They were the most horrifying images of human slaughter, ritualistic killings, and mutilation she couldn't even imagine. She saw images of a cult, satin worshippers, mass murder, torture, and mutilation of adults and children. Jolynn gasped at the gruesomeness of what she witnessed and flew backward several feet, unable to take her eyes off the dead man in the casket. Her horrified expression told it all.

"He's trying to raise the demon," Jolynn gasped without looking away. "That's his mentor. Some deranged monster he idolized years ago."

"Please, let's go," Gillian begged softly almost down to tears of fright.

The candles flickered, yet there was no draft. Both women gasped and looked around with concern. Jolynn moved closer to the casket and again peered at the decayed man. The corpse's eyes suddenly opened. Jolynn screamed and bolted backwards, nearly knocking over Gillian, who screamed because Jolynn did. Upon a second look, his eyes were still closed, but her vision was enough to rattle her. Several candles suddenly flickered and extinguished. Both screamed again and ran from the room.

Chapter Forty-three

Gillian headed into the kitchen and ran for the door leading to the hallway. Jolynn caught her arm, stopping her, and firmly indicated the basement door. Gillian appeared horrified while staring at her moderately deranged friend.

"Are you out of your mind?" she practically cried out. "I'm not going down there!"

"I came in through the basement door in the fruit cellar," Jolynn informed her. "There's a good chance it's not on the same control as the other doors."

Gillian considered the comment, fidgeted with fright, and then groaned with frustration. "I know I'm going to live to regret this," she muttered then sighed. "But it won't be long, since we're both going to die shortly after."

They hurried through the basement door and quickly but quietly headed down the rickety steps. Once they reached the bottom, Jolynn guided Gillian through the furnace room and into the fruit cellar, hurrying her to the door near the back. They reached the old door, which she had originally left open, but it was now closed. Jolynn stared at the closed door with concern, held her breath a moment, and then attempted to open the door. Neither were surprised that it wouldn't budge. There would be little point to attempting to kick it open, since the door opened inward. Jolynn held her head while attempting to come up with a plan as she looked around the windowless fruit cellar.

"There must be a master switch for the electronic locking mechanism on the doors," Jolynn informed her friend. "Logically, it'd be located down here."

"We don't even know where to look," Gillian protested. "It's too dark down here. It'll take us forever to find your switch-- providing it even exists."

Jolynn considered the comment while trying to remain calm. "Then we'll have to find another way out."

She pulled Gillian toward the furnace room. Undetected by either woman, a shadow emerged from another section of the basement. Jolynn and Gillian hurried into the furnace room and nearly stumbled over something lying on the floor just off to the side. Jolynn shined her flashlight at the floor. Both stared with horror at Carl's butchered body then screamed. Without hesitation or rational thinking, they ran for the rickety steps and headed up them. Gillian's foot broke through one of the rotted boards with a loud crack and her foot became wedged between the jagged wood. Jolynn frantically attempted to pull her friend's foot free.

They saw a shadow move within the firewood storage area only a few yards away. He'd heard them, and they were stuck without a prayer. Gillian clutched the machete and attempted to keep an eye on the area where they'd seen the shadow while Jolynn pulled on Gillian's leg, attempting to free her foot from the splintered wooden step. The Pen Pal's silhouette was now seen in the opening. Gillian screamed. Jolynn didn't bother looking up and pulled frantically to free her friend.

The Pen Pal stepped into the light, revealing his creepy bloodstained mask, raised his dagger in a deadly fashion, and walked toward them with a morbid confidence. He knew they were trapped, and he appeared eager to savor the moment. Jolynn quickly straightened and aggressively stomped on the broken board. It splinted with each thrust while both women screamed for different reasons. As soon as the board gave away just enough, Gillian pulled her foot free. Jolynn removed the gun from her shoulder holster and aimed it at the approaching killer. Before she could pull the trigger, he darted back into the darkness. Jolynn twitched while giving serious consideration to chasing after the notorious killer. Gillian must have sensed her friend's unpredictable mood and grabbed her arm, pulling her up the stairs behind her.

Gillian threw open the kitchen door, causing it to strike the opposing wall with a loud crack. They wasted little time bolting through the opening. Both women nearly collided with Slade. Gillian screamed and swung the machete. Slade jumped back as the machete struck the wall. He eyed the machete that nearly struck him then looked at Gillian and Jolynn. Jolynn slammed the basement door shut and placed a brace across it.

"You just don't listen," Slade announced then pulled them toward the outer kitchen door. "Take her to the car. Wait for us there."

"Slade--" she protested.

"Not another word."

Slade attempted to open the door and appeared surprised when it didn't budge. He pulled harder with frustration.

"What the hell?"

"He electronically locked the doors and windows somehow," Jolynn informed him. "He wants to make sure we're stuck inside his fun house."

"That monster's down there," Gillian cried out while pointing to the basement door.

Slade assessed the outer door and nearby windows but quickly came to the same defeated conclusion. "Damn it," he grumbled. "We'll need to find a way to break through the boards on the windows."

"Boards nothing," Gillian cried out while indicating the windows. "I see metal plates. We're sealed inside with that maniac."

"There must be a master switch for the locks," Jolynn informed them.

"I really want to go home now," Gillian insisted.

Jolynn set the gun on the counter and removed the pendant necklace from her pocket. "Give me five minutes," Jolynn announced.

Jolynn sat in the corner of the kitchen, clutched the pendant between both hands, and shut her eyes.

Gillian stared at her friend with surprise then eyed Slade. "What's she doing?" she almost demanded.

Slade snatched Jolynn's gun from the countertop and handed it to Gillian, who uncertainly accepted it. He glanced briefly at Jolynn and drew a deep breath. "She's finding a way out, I hope."

Gillian set the machete down on the counter and checked over the gun she now held.

Slade gave her a stern, serious look. "I have three friends in this house," he informed her. "Watch your targets and try not to shoot my friends." He briefly glanced at Jolynn where she meditated in the corner. "Time to regroup." He touched his ear transmitter. "We have the girl. Meet me in the kitchen," he informed the others. "We lost our way out, and we need a new extraction plan. Our friend was last seen in the basement."

"Negative," Wilson announced through his ear transmitter. "He's on his way upstairs. We're right behind him." There was a brief pause. "Baxter, he's heading upstairs. Cut him off."

"Copy," Baxter responded through the ear transmitter. "On my way."

"Don't lose him," Slade responded to his men. "I have Jolynn and Gillian in the kitchen. I'll work on opening this place for our exit." He turned to Gillian with a look of irritation. "I thought you said he was in the basement?"

"He was; I swear," Gillian practically cried out. "He came after us!"

"This place must be loaded with secret passageways," he announced and shook his head with disgust. "We're stuck in his satanic playground now." He tapped his ear transmitter. "Guys, proceed with caution. This place is crawling with secret passageways. He could be anywhere."

Chapter Forty-four

Wilson and Rush entered the second floor hallway from the main staircase and looked around the quiet, front hall. There wasn't any sign of Baxter, although he was supposed to be upstairs. They exchanged concerned looks.

"Baxter," Wilson said through his ear transmitter, so as not to disclose their location to the killer, if he was nearby. "What's your location?"

There was no response. Both men again exchanged concerned looks.

"Second floor in the back hallway near the rear stairs," Baxter finally responded through the ear transmitter. "No sign of him anywhere."

"He could be in any of the rooms," Wilson informed him. "Watch your back."

"Way ahead of you, as usual," came his response.

Within the back hallway, Baxter cautiously passed several darkened rooms while keeping his gun aimed and an eye out for any movement. A door just a few feet away from him swayed gently. Baxter aimed his gun at the door and approached with caution. He pushed the door open while keeping his gun aimed and remained to the side of the doorway. He aimed his flashlight into the bedroom and strained to look into the darkened room. He suddenly cringed and wrinkled his nose at the foul stench.

"Holy hell," he gasped softly while attempting to block out the smell with his hand. "What a smell--"

A floorboard creaked behind him, forcing him to spin with his gun aimed. Despite the sound he'd heard within the hallway, there was no one there. Baxter appeared puzzled then became concerned. As he turned back for the opening with his gun aimed, the Pen Pal stood in the darkened doorway and plunged his dagger into Baxter's shoulder, missing his back by a split second. Baxter cried out with surprise and agony while firing his gun, although he hadn't taken time to aim. As the knife was pulled from his shoulder, Baxter took aim. The Pen Pal grabbed his hand holding the gun and tackled Baxter across the hall. They crashed into the opposing wall. The gun fired again as Baxter struck the wall with a loud thud. The Pen Pal snarled and repeatedly stabbed Baxter in the chest, his decorative dagger easily piercing through flesh and bone. Baxter only managed one terrified scream, incapacitated from the first strike, and was unable to defend himself to any of the following blows.

✝

Jolynn remained quietly sitting in the corner of the kitchen with the pendant clutched in her hands. She hadn't moved or made a sound since she placed herself in the corner. Slade held his finger to his ear transmitter and listened to what was happening, his horrified expression telling the story. Gillian watched his reaction while wrenching her fingers together. Even Gillian had heard Baxter's first and final scream through Slade's ear transmitter.

"Baxter?" Slade helplessly called out through the transmitter. "Baxter, answer me." There was no response, although neither had expected one. "Wilson? Rush? Did you find Baxter?"

There was a long silence. Gillian moved closer to Slade while staring at him, the horror showing on her face.

"Wilson? Rush? Do you copy?"

"Yeah, Slade," Wilson announced with disgust in his voice. "We found Baxter." There was a moment of hesitation. "He's dead."

"We need to find this fucker," Rush shouted through the transmitter, his anger rising.

Slade began pacing while keeping his finger to his ear. His anger at the entire situation was evident as well. "Get down here right away." Slade continued his conversation with the guys while looking at Gillian. "We're leaving."

"Slade, are you sure you want to do that?" Rush questioned. "We may never get this close again. We can't just walk away. He's going to come back. You know that."

"This place is crawling with secret passages. He could be anywhere," Slade informed them, sharing their frustration. "I saw some kerosene cans downstairs. I say we blow this place with him in it."

Gillian leaped closer to Slade and touched his arm, concern in her eyes. "We can't even get out," she protested.

"Get down here," Slade informed the others then turned to Gillian. "Leave that to me."

"Oh, I don't like the sound of that," Gillian gasped as her eyes widened with fear.

"The switch for the locks must be in the basement somewhere," Slade informed them. "That's where you said you last saw him just before the doors locked. I'll find the switch." He looked at Jolynn, who remained silently in the corner without having moved. It's possible she hadn't heard any of their conversation. Slade drew a deep breath then looked back at Gillian. "As soon as the doors unlock, I want you and Jolynn to head for the cars toward the front of the house."

Gillian stared at him with a look of horror on her face. Slade approached the basement door without further comment. Gillian hurried across the kitchen and stopped him.

"You can't go down there," Gillian gasped. "You don't know this guy. He'll kill you."

"Trust me," Slade informed her. "I know exactly what I'm up against."

Slade easily pulled away from her and continued toward the door. Gillian looked back at Jolynn in the corner of the kitchen and pointed demandingly back at Slade as he passed through the basement door.

"Jolynn, stop him!"

Jolynn didn't respond. It seemed as if she hadn't even heard her. Gillian stared at her friend with disbelief. Slade disappeared into the basement.

"Great rescue," Gillian muttered while throwing her hands in the air. "I'm practically alone again."

✝

Slade walked slowly down the basement steps with his gun in his hand. When he reached the bottom, he discovered Carl's body had vanished. He looked around with surprise. Moving the body seemed unnecessary. Slade silently walked past the large pool of blood remaining on the floor, the only reminder of Carl's ultimate sacrifice, and cautiously approached the basement storage room not far from him.

Chapter Forty-five

Jolynn remained in the corner of the kitchen in her hypnotic state with the pendant clutched in her hands. She hadn't spoken or moved since she took up residence in the corner. Gillian paced the kitchen while wrenching her fingers together, occasionally casting looks at her unresponsive friend.

"Shit," Gillian muttered insecurely. "I wish I would have stayed in bed."

Jolynn suddenly gasped and opened her eyes, startling her friend. Gillian spun on her heels, ran for Jolynn in the corner, and pulled her to her feet. Jolynn jerked with surprise then gently pulled away from her friend and looked around the kitchen.

"Where's Slade?"

"The cavalry went downstairs to find the master switch for the doors," Gillian remarked. "What the hell, Jolynn? What's going on? How could you just zone out like that?"

It was almost as if Jolynn didn't hear a word her friend had said. The look on her face expressed her horror. "The monster--" she gasped then looked at Gillian with frightening unpredictability. "I have to help Slade."

"You're out of your mind!"

"I know where the switch is," Jolynn insisted. "It's in the furnace room. There's a lever against the wall near a secret passageway."

"How could you possibly know that?" Gillian almost demanded.

"Trust me."

"Trust you?" Gillian gasped with horror. "To do what? Get yourself killed?"

They heard someone coming down the back kitchen stairs. Gillian appeared relieved and turned toward the rear staircase.

"Thank God," Gillian groaned softly. "Maybe we can get out of here now."

Gillian approached the back stairs with Jolynn directly behind her. The Pen Pal appeared on the stairs and lunged for Gillian with his dagger. Gillian screamed and jumped away from the slashing blade while attempting to raise the gun at the same time. The Pen Pal backhanded her across the face and knocked her to the floor. The gun flew across the kitchen floor toward the back stairs. Jolynn lunged for her discarded machete on the counter. The Pen Pal swung the knife at her and struck the counter just inches from her fingers. Jolynn screamed and jumped backward, having narrowly lost her fingers. She ran for Gillian, pulled her to her feet, and hurried her toward the connecting dining room door.

Gillian and Jolynn ran into the dining room, pausing only a moment to see a panel pulled away from the wall, indicating a secret passageway. With the killer directly behind them, they knew the passageway would be safe. They ran to the opening and darted into the candlelit room. Gillian slammed the passageway door behind them and looked around for something to brace it shut. When Gillian turned, she saw the horrified look on Jolynn's face and followed her gaze to the center of the room.

Candles surrounded the center of the room revealing the week-old, decaying remains of a redhead woman sprawled across the worn, sage fainting couch. The dead woman's body crawled with bugs and rats, making it hard to tell where the couch began and the mutilated body ended. Jolynn and Gillian stared at the dead woman, unable to identify her due to the severe decay. The secret passageway door opened behind them to reveal the Pen Pal. Both women saw him at the same time, screamed, and ran across the room for what looked like a connecting door. The Pen Pal caught Jolynn by the shirt and slung her onto the fainting couch, sending the decayed woman and dozens of rats crashing to the floor. In the split second, Jolynn saw the woman as she was in life, catching a glimpse of her face. She saw the woman with Dan rolling around naked in bed together. Another flash revealed the woman fighting with Heidi at the tavern. The flashes ended just as quickly as they had begun, returning Jolynn to a terrifying reality.

The Pen Pal hovered over Jolynn, who was half lying on the fainting couch with a few rats scurrying across her body. He clutched her throat and held her to the couch with one hand while raising the bloodied dagger with the other. Jolynn thrashed wildly with her legs while attempting to hold back the hand clutching the knife and loosen the grip on her throat at the same time. Horrifying images flashed through her mind. She saw scenes of his childhood, as a young boy chasing a little girl with a knife and slaughtering defenseless animals. Gillian cried out while leaping onto the Pen Pal's back and attempted to choke him with her forearm. Gillian rode his back while kicking and screaming like a wild woman.

"Let her go," Gillian cried out in a shrill voice. "Let her go, you bastard!"

Jolynn gasped for air, feeling weak and dizzy. She could feel herself slipping into unconsciousness as a dark haze clouded her vision. The Pen Pal seemed to have the same problem with Gillian's arm around his neck. She had a sharp hold across his throat, which he couldn't break without releasing his victim. Rush and Wilson called out to them from the kitchen. The Pen Pal suddenly straightened while pulling Jolynn from the couch by her throat. Despite her excellent hold and best bull riding leg lock, Gillian was thrown from his back. She flew across the room and forcibly struck the wall near the passageway door. Her pain from the hard hit was evident as she gasped and started to sink to the floor. Beyond his mask, the Pen Pal stared into Jolynn's eyes and smiled through sharpened teeth with a look of satisfaction as she choked beneath his hands.

She stared into his eyes beyond the creepy mask as the images continued to flash. She finally saw images of herself from his life, images within the medical records department. They faded away to different images, those of the future. She saw a vision of Slade repeatedly stabbed by the Pen Pal then watched as he died a horrific death. Jolynn's eyes burned with rage. She attempted to scream with anger, although nothing came out. She rammed her knee into the Pen Pal's groin. He immediately released her and doubled over. Jolynn gasped to catch her breath only a moment before grabbing a nearby brass candlestick. The candle few from the stick as she struck the Pen Pal over the head with it, dazing him.

"I won't let you do it," she cried out. "I won't let you kill him!" She reached down and grabbed the hair attached to his mask and pulled with all her strength as she cried out. "No more, Mr. McQueen!"

The mask came off to reveal her boss, McQueen, kneeling on the floor before her. He stared at her a moment, somehow knowing she'd figure it out. A strange, twisted smile full of sharply filed teeth crossed his demented face. The teeth were his own. He only wore dentures to conceal what he had done to his real teeth.

"What did you see, Jolynn?" he snarled softly. "Did you see your boyfriend's heart in my hand?" McQueen chuckled the most evil laugh she'd ever heard.

She stared at him with horror then anger. "That woman was your wife," she gasped while indicating the dead woman on the floor. "You killed your wife!"

"That cheating bitch had to die," he informed her with a sneer on his face. "It was bad enough she was running around on her business trips with any man she could find, but her and Dan? That's when I knew she had to die. It couldn't have worked out better. Thanks to your new friend, everyone is going to believe Dan is the killer."

"You sick fuck!"

"Me?" he demanded then laughed. "You were the one fucking that wannabe federal agent. I knew who he was the moment I saw him at your desk." He grinned through his sharpened teeth. "I remember his sister *very* well. It was a tough decision, you know. I really wanted to take him out first that morning in your apartment. It would have been so satisfying, and he would have been so easy to kill in the shower." He laughed again while raising his evil brows. "He invited me in thinking it was you outside the bathroom. I could have slit his throat before he knew what happened, but I chose you first. You've been a thorn in my side since the day you were hired. So beautiful yet so snarly." His grin cheapened. "The thought of tearing your throat out and drinking your blood while it was still warm had me hot and bothered every time I saw you."

Horror crossed her face, but it was immediately followed by rage. Jolynn cried out and struck him again with the candlestick at the same time he slashed at her with his dagger, slicing her thigh. Jolynn cried out with pain and surprise. Despite his bleeding head, McQueen straightened and attempted to slash her again. Gillian grabbed Jolynn and pulled her out of the weapon's path and toward the secret entrance. McQueen bolted across the room in the opposite direction. He obviously knew something they didn't, but neither woman was about to run after him to find out what that was.

✝

Wilson and Rush approached the connecting dining room door from the kitchen. The door flew open and struck Wilson as Jolynn and Gillian bolted into the safety of the kitchen. Gillian screamed when she saw the unfamiliar men then must have realized they were the rest of Slade's rescue party. She frantically pointed to the dining room.

"He's in a secret room just beyond the dining room," Gillian screamed.

"It's my boss, Mr. McQueen," Jolynn cried out. "I saw him!"

Rush and Wilson ran into the dining room with their weapons raised. Jolynn grabbed the machete and suddenly bolted for the basement door, knowing she had to reach Slade. Gillian watched in horror as her friend passed through the doorway.

"Jo, no!"

Jolynn disappeared into the stairway and thundered down the rickety stairs. Gillian ran her fingers through her hair while spinning around frustrated and frightened, uncertain what to do now that she was once again alone. She clutched her head then looked at the basement stairs as if contemplating something unthinkable.

"Damn it," Gillian groaned softly. "I'm going to need months of therapy."

Gillian looked around the kitchen for a weapon or anything useful. Near the back stairs, she saw the discarded gun lying on the floor. She pounced on the gun, straightened, and held it against her chest for comfort.

Chapter Forty-six

Slade entered the dimly lit basement storage room containing a few candles for an added creepy effect. He looked around in silent observation. For an abandoned house, there was an abundance of clutter in the basement. He looked from the candles to the kerosene cans on the floor near the back of the dimly lit room. The presence of the flammable liquid was curious in itself, but Slade didn't have time to overthink it.

"There you are," he softly remarked and hurried for the kerosene cans.

As he approached, he caught a glimpse of the Pen Pal in the corner, sitting in a chair alongside a propane tank. Slade jumped with surprise and aimed his gun at the killer in the creepy clown mask. The killer didn't move. Slade stared at him a moment longer then noticed the fresh blood collecting beneath the chair. Slade slowly and uncertainly approached the killer in the chair. His abdomen was saturated in fresh blood, indicating he was clearly dead. Slade's eyes narrowed with a confused look. He kept his gun aimed and reached for the killer's mask. He hesitated only a moment before ripping the mask from his face revealing Dan. Slade stared at the dead young man and attempted to process what he was seeing. Then it came to him.

"You were never the killer," Slade announced softly under his breath. "You were the scapegoat."

The candles within the room flickered, indicating a gust of air in an otherwise sealed room. It could only mean one thing. Slade quickly spun around, and he was immediately tackled to the floor by the now unmasked killer. Slade landed roughly on his back with McQueen on top of him, his gun sliding across the room and between the kerosene cans. Slade stared at McQueen pinning him to the floor while holding his decorative dagger. The serial killer's true identity was startling to him. McQueen attempted to stab him in the throat while Slade struggled to keep the dagger away from his face.

As they wrestled in a power struggle for the dagger, McQueen lunged for Slade's throat with his sharpened teeth. Slade cried out with horror and clutched McQueen's throat with his right hand to hold him back. A faint male voice was heard calling through Slade's earpiece. It was Wilson attempting to contact him. He was unable to respond to Wilson's call. Slade was losing the battle of strength with gravity and the killer's weight working against him. McQueen's sharpened teeth came dangerously close to Slade's throat.

"Slade," Wilson again cried out through his ear transmitter. "What's your location? We've lost him!"

Slade thrust his forehead into McQueen's nose, momentarily stunning the killer with a painful blow. Slade cried out as he tossed the man off him but only managed to throw him a mere foot or two. Slade scrambled to his feet as McQueen moved to his knees and snarled like a wild animal. Slade kicked him in the face, tossing him backward with surprising force. Jolynn ran into the room with the machete in her hand and slid to a stop. She was only two feet from the frightening killer, who now stood before her. Slade's expression immediately dropped when he saw her.

"Jo, get out of here!"

Jolynn heard his plea, but from where she was standing, it wasn't really an option. He'd be on top of her before she could even turn. She attempted to back away from McQueen, needing more room to swing. McQueen leaped for her and grabbed her by the throat, causing the machete to fall from her hand. She immediately clutched the hand holding her throat. McQueen coiled back with the dagger to his hip, preparing to thrust it into her midsection. Slade bolted for Jolynn and McQueen.

"No!"

Possibly having seen him out of the corner of his eye, McQueen cast Jolynn across the room and slashed at Slade with the dagger. Jolynn slid across the floor several feet away looking slightly dazed. Slade jumped from the dagger's path, spun into a roundhouse kick, and struck McQueen in the chest. McQueen staggered back a step but quickly recovered and returned for another attack with the dagger. Slade grabbed the wrist holding the dagger and attempted to keep it from striking him. He kicked McQueen several times in the side, but he didn't have enough force to faze him. The knife scratched Slade's arm. Slade cried out and jumped back a step. McQueen thrust the decorative dagger for Slade's throat. It clashed against the mildly rusted machete with a loud clang. Slade caught a glimpse of Jolynn, who stood directly before him with the machete in her hand. McQueen glared at Jolynn with irritation to her constant interference.

Jolynn's look was harsh and cold. She no longer showed fear for the killer. Both pulled their weapons back. McQueen slashed at her, making the first aggressive move. Jolynn cried out with anger and hatred as she thrust her machete forward. McQueen's dagger sliced through her shirt and some skin. The machete impaled McQueen's abdomen, leaving him stunned. He possibly never imagined a victim getting the upper hand on him, particularly this one. He staggered back as she pulled the old machete free. McQueen held his bleeding abdomen, maintaining his startled look, and backed away from her. Slade and Jolynn stared at him without remorse. To their surprise, he didn't fall. McQueen found the strength to turn and stumble from the room. Jolynn gasped with surprise then became angry and ran after him.

"Jolynn, no!"

Jolynn entered the next room with Slade directly behind her. McQueen was gone! Both witnessed a passageway door closing securely in place. Jolynn ran for the secret passageway door and slammed her palm against it with frustration. She looked at the lever just alongside the hidden door. She knew what it was and pulled it. She heard the same electronic hum followed by a click. It wasn't the passageway lever but the controls that kept them locked inside the house. She'd unlocked the doors! Slade looked around with the same realization then turned to Jolynn.

"Let's get the hell out of here." He then touched his ear transmitter. "The doors are open," Slade announced to the others. "Everyone out. We're blowing this clambake."

Slade grabbed Jolynn's hand and pulled her from the furnace room. Slade and Jolynn entered the fruit cellar and nearly collided with Gillian. Both Gillian and Jolynn let out startled screams then relaxed. Slade hurried them to the fruit cellar door and the only basement exit. They were about to leave when Slade hesitated before the door and touched his ear transmitter.

"Everyone out?"

"Copy," Wilson was heard over the transmitter. "We're heading out the kitchen door now."

He turned to the women with a serious look on his face. "Get to the car," he announced firmly. "I'll be a minute behind you."

"Slade--" Jolynn protested.

"Just go," he ordered.

Gillian grabbed Jolynn's hand. "Come on, Jo," she screamed and pulled her from the basement.

Slade ran into the furnace room, approached the kerosene cans, and retrieved his gun. He kicked over one of the containers, spilling kerosene across the floor. Slade removed one of the nearby candles and tossed it to the floor. He casually turned and left the room as the kerosene ignited and swiftly raced for the cans and the nearby propane tank, engulfing it in flames.

Chapter Forty-seven

Jolynn and Gillian hurried from the cellar doorway and toward the old shed rather than run all the way to the car and van. They turned a few feet away from the shed and waited anxiously for Slade who was only supposed to be a minute behind them. There was a brief moment of anticipation. Slade finally appeared from the fruit cellar entrance and approached them in no particular hurry. He stopped halfway and turned to face the house, casually placing his hands in his pockets.

"For you, Angie. With love."

The house suddenly exploded into a ball of fire with debris flying everywhere. What little remained of the house swiftly burned. Gillian and Jolynn were halfway to the ground to the sound of the massive explosion. They slowly straightened from alongside the shed. McQueen suddenly darted out from behind a large tree and tackled Slade to the ground. Jolynn screamed and hurried toward them with the machete in her hands. Slade swiftly tossed McQueen off him. Both scrambled to their feet. McQueen lunged for Slade with his dagger and a newly found rage despite his severe injury. Jolynn raised the machete, prepared to take his head off. A gunshot suddenly rang out. McQueen was stopped mid-stride, his head snapping back as the bullet penetrated directly between his eyes. His eyes rolled back as he fell backwards to the ground, the decorative dagger falling from his outstretched hand. Jolynn and Slade quickly turned, looking behind them. Gillian lowered the gun from only a few feet away with a sneer on her face. She casually tossed the gun aside.

"There's my fucking therapy," she snarled.

Slade pulled Jolynn into his arms and held her in a tight embrace. She dropped the machete and returned the hug. Wilson and Rush hurried past what was left of the burning building, having heard the gunshot. Jolynn and Slade looked back at the dead man lying on the ground. Jolynn glanced alongside her and saw the reaper standing by her side. They stared at each other a moment in silent conversation. The reaper turned toward the dead man and slashed downward with his sling blade, penetrating the dead man's chest with his ghostly weapon. He dragged the blade back, pulling the Pen Pal's soul from his body. McQueen's soul struggled against the blade as it ripped him from his earthly body. The Pen Pal's soul erupted into flames then evaporated into the ground. The reaper straightened proudly, having done his job, and disappeared. Jolynn felt a strange, twisted smile cross her face.

"Let's have a moment of silence for Baxter and Carl," Slade announced to the men.

Everyone lowered their heads and silently reflected their fallen team members. Their victory was marred by the death of their men, but they knew Baxter and Carl would rest better knowing they had been avenged.

Rush was the first to lift his head and look around at the others. He drew a deep breath then offered a twisted smile. "Well, no point in wasting a good fire."

Slade nodded and gestured to the dead man on the ground. All three men grabbed the Pen Pal's body and dragged him to the burning house. Gillian and Jolynn glanced at each other then hugged happily, hiding their tears of joy and relief that it was finally over. After a long embrace, they pulled away and watched the three men throw the killer's body into the flames.

"We don't need to watch this if you'd rather not," Jolynn gently informed her friend.

"Are you kidding?" Gillian squawked cheerfully and offered a devious smile. "I want to roast marshmallows and sing camping songs."

Jolynn was slightly surprised by her friend's macabre sense of humor, but she certainly couldn't blame her. She offered her own smile and refrained from chuckling at the comment. Gillian's look then turned serious as she folded her arms across her chest while staring at her friend.

"Seriously though. How *did* you find me?" she finally asked then indicated the three men by the bonfire. "And who are those guys?"

"That's a very long, complicated story," Jolynn informed her while maintaining her smile. "I'm just glad you're back in one-piece."

"I had my doubts for a while. I couldn't help thinking I should have just gone to work," Gillian remarked while forcing a smile.

"I doubt that would have changed the outcome," Jolynn replied. "He targeted you. Home or at work, he still would have come after you."

"I was thinking the same thing too," she replied. "I can't believe your boss was the creep who was hitting on me at the bar the other night. I'm guessing he didn't just want to kill me because I rejected him."

"No, it goes much deeper than that," Jolynn replied. "He was part of a cult years ago. When his leader died, he tried to live a normal life. I guess when he found out his wife was cheating on him, he slipped back into insanity and started killing women who looked like her."

"You're saying your boss was a retired psychopath?" Gillian questioned with surprise.

"Yes," she replied softly then sighed. "He just came out of retirement."

"How do you know all this?" Gillian again asked.

Jolynn offered a warm smile. "I'm afraid I have some secrets I've been keeping too."

Gillian stared at her with moderate alarm. "You weren't in on that cult, were you?"

"No, of course not," she gasped then held her breath and cringed at the words she dreaded saying aloud. "I'm, uh, sort of psychic."

Gillian stared at her with a hard to read look on her face. "Oh, well, that explains a lot."

Jolynn stared at her with surprise. "You actually believe me?"

Her friend shrugged. "Come on, Jo," she announced with little concern. "You're pretty strange. I knew there had to be something going on with you. I'm just glad you finally decided to tell me."

Jolynn stared at her with disbelief then allowed a soft laugh to escape her throat. "That's a switch."

Slade approached them, leaving Rush and Wilson by the bonfire while dancing a celebratory hoedown. Slade's smile beamed as he hugged Jolynn and then kissed her quickly on the lips. Gillian stared at them with a look of disbelief.

"Now I know I've missed something," she muttered.

Jolynn took Slade's hand and proudly turned toward her friend. "Gillian, I'd like you to meet Harris Slade."

Slade smiled and shook Gillian's hand. "It's been an adventure trying to meet you."

"I'm glad you were determined," Gillian teased then released his hand and suspiciously eyed her friend. "So what's going on here? You finally decide to start dating while I'm in the hands of a psycho killer?"

"It was fate that brought us together," he informed Gillian then glanced at Jolynn with a strange look. "A fate you yourself altered. What happened to fulfilling one's destiny and that tragic lover bullshit?"

Jolynn hid her smile and casually shrugged. "I considered it, but where's the fun in that?"

Slade pulled her to his side and held her while smiling with a look of satisfaction. "I think I'll take you home with me," he teased. "We'll live a quiet, secluded life together."

Gillian stared at them with her mouth hanging open. "You're going to just leave me after what I've been through?" she nearly gasped.

"You can come along," Slade informed her without hesitation. "The staff enjoy houseguests."

"Staff? He has staff?" Gillian gasped while looking at her friend with surprise. "Where'd you find this guy? Hiding in medical records?"

Jolynn held back her laugh. "Actually, yes."

Gillian stared at her with a baffled look, uncertain whether she was actually serious.

Slade clung to Jolynn, inhaled deeply, and breathed a sigh of relief. "After over a year of relentless pursuit of the Pen Pal, it's finally over," he announced. "I'm finally free. Angie can rest in peace."

Jolynn placed her arms around Slade's neck and clung to him. He held her against him as if he'd never let go. In the near distance, Rush and Wilson continued their hoedown in front of the burning farmhouse.

The End

Other books by Holly Copella!
Reviews left on Amazon are appreciated!

"The Battle for Andrea Marie"

A cruise ship attack turns six survivors into overnight celebrities after they take credit for the heroic act of a stowaway who died saving them.

The cruise is just what Jess needed--a bit of harmless fun far from her daily grind. But what begins as a relaxing vacation turns into a desperate fight for her life when terrorists take over the ship and start piling up bodies. Teaming up with a mysterious stowaway, Jess attempts to send out a distress call but knows they cannot wait for help to come. If she or the few remaining passengers have any hope for survival, Jess must act now. The papers dub it "The Battle for *Andrea Marie*," but to Jess it is the moment she fought side-by-side with her enigmatic Romeo, saving the ship--and losing him. She thinks the story ends there, but really, the nightmare is just beginning...

"Insanely Deadly"

When the dead return to life, it's up to an admiral's daughter and a mildly insane, former war hero to save their small town.

Jetta Cross, a Navy Admiral's daughter, is tasked with keeping her father's comrade, a former war hero turned town crazy, grounded in the real world. Capt. John Hunter is still fighting the war in his head, where imaginary dead people are part of his world. When a viral outbreak brings about a zombie uprising, Hunter is left to his own devices. He must resume his role as a one-man commando unit in order to destroy the ravenous undead. With Hunter still fighting his own inner demons as well as the undead, the townspeople fear their zombie neighbors may not be the only threat. Stranded at the island's luxurious resort with a handful of workers, Jetta is forced to live up to her father's reputation and take charge of the deteriorating situation at the hotel. She must wage her own war against the infected before the government declares her hometown a total loss.

"Deadly Institution"

A town recluse suspected of killing his wife teams up with a young woman in order to stop a killer.

After being accused of murdering his wife, Konrad Asher turns his back on the town that once adored him. Ten years later, he still holds his grudge and the title of the most feared man in town. With the reopening of the burned mental institution, where his wife had died, former employees are now murdered one-by-one, throwing suspicion back on Asher. A young local reporter, Jacey, is forced to reveal her long-time friendship with the infamous recluse in order to clear his name not only in the recent murders but to exonerate him in the death of his wife as well. Will Jacey's relationship with Asher invite the killer closer to her? Or is the killer already in her life?

"Screenplays: The Island Collection"
"Jungle Princess", "A.L.F. Resort", "Brighton Island"

Discover how romance and fun in the sun can be downright *chilling*!

"Jungle Princess" is a romantic/thriller that leaves a teenage girl stranded on an island with two male shipmates and a creature of "unknown" origin. She soon discovers the island is home to an abandoned prison with several prisoners roaming free. What really killed over one hundred prisoners? And is it still out there--?

"A.L.F. Resort" is a romantic/thriller set on an island resort with Artificial Life Forms as the main draw. At this resort, all your fantasies come true...until a malfunction removes safety inhibitors on the A.L.F.'s. Zombies, biker gangs, and mobsters run amuck, turning fantasies into nightmares. A young reporter gets more of a story than she anticipates, but will she survive long enough to write the story?

"Brighton Island" is a romantic/thriller set on a private island. When the owner's niece brings her psychic friend to the mansion, his presence awakens the spirits' tortured souls. As the psychic attempts to solve the old murders, the niece is confronted with the possibility that she's next to join the mansion ghosts. Stranded on the island with a crazed killer, her uncle wages his own war to save them. Will his "shock and awe" tactics actually save them or get them killed?

"Reaper of Souls"
A fantasy short story

A young woman must outwit an evil sorcerer in order to save her brother or become one of his minions forever.

Unwilling to believe her brother is dead, Reggie discovers an underhanded deal made with Kahn, a less than ethical sorcerer, who collects humans to serve as slaves in his kingdom. In order to rescue her brother from his horrible fate, she must complete his failed task or be forced to serve Kahn forever. After being transported to his world, Reggie realizes that even if she beats Kahn at his own game, she's at his mercy for him to uphold his end of the deal. All seems lost until Kahn's discontented, self-serving brother, Helsing, arrives. Can Reggie convince Helsing to help her? And at what cost?

"Death Displacement"

A grief-stricken man travels back in time to seek revenge on the woman who murdered his girlfriend but inadvertently falls in love with her.

Kane is about to marry the woman he loves. His life is perfect. A few weeks before the wedding, a vindictive woman from his girlfriend's past mysteriously arrives and kills her. He learns of a traumatic accident that happened five years earlier, which triggers Riley's hatred for his girlfriend. Distraught over his girlfriend's death, Kane uses an antique time machine to travel into the past in order to find and destroy the woman responsible. When he runs into Riley's younger self, he realizes she's not the monster she later becomes, and he can't bring himself to destroy her. With a little help from his oddball friend from the past, they formulate a plan to prevent the accident that sends Riley down her destructive path. Kane's plan backfires when he falls for the younger Riley. His new tortured existence is further complicated when future Riley, his girlfriend's killer, shows up with her own devious agenda that doesn't include him. Will he be able to stop the time ripple, which ultimately ends with his girlfriend's death? Or will future Riley take him out of the timeline forever--

"Dead Village"

After strange happenings isolate a small resort town from the rest of the world, nearly one hundred residents seek refuge at the closed hotel. Only eight survive the night. And that's just the beginning...

One day after the entire population of Fox Ridge Village disappears, a car wreck forces several unsuspecting crash victims to seek help at the closed summer hotel. Within the hotel, they discover the grisly aftermath of a brutal slaughter. Crash victims Vander and Devon, a reluctant clairvoyant, team up to solve the riddle of the "haunted hotel" and the mass hysteria plaguing the remaining survivors. By the time they discover the hotel's secret, they're already drawn into the hysteria. As the body count continues to climb, it's a race to isolate the source and bring everyone back to reality before they kill one another. Will Devon be able to communicate with the traumatized spirits before their fate becomes her own?

"Misfits, Inc."

A seemingly ordinary, young woman meets four misfits who claim she has given them supernatural powers.

While on a business trip to a remote island paradise, a bored secretary, Hailey, has her world turned upside down when her path collides with a psychic freak, Skyler. He attempts to convince her that they had met in his dreams, and she had chosen him as one of her four mystic warriors. After Skyler foresees a woman's death, they discover an unidentified creature has killed one of the guests. They are joined by a lounge pianist and a rich playboy, who also claim they had met her in their dreams. If Skyler's prophecies are genuine, the evil entity controlling the ravenous creatures needs to destroy Hailey to ensure its survival. Reluctantly accepting her fate, Hailey has to locate the last and most powerful of her chosen warriors, The Guardian. Their fate is in doubt when The Guardian turns out to be a self-absorbed, former cat burglar with a bad attitude. Can Hailey turn her company of misfits into an elite team of mystic warriors? Or will The Guardian's secret agenda destroy them all?

"Basement Dwellers"

A viral outbreak at a hospital leaves a mortician, sheriff, and coroner fighting for their lives against a horde of undead and the CDC.

After a massive car wreck leaves several survivors in critical condition at the local hospital, a surgeon uses experimental drugs on his critical patients and accidentally causes a zombie outbreak. When local mortician, Lexx, receives an infected corpse as her client, she becomes stranded in the hospital basement during CDC quarantine along with the local sheriff and the coroner. The infamous surgeon struggles to find a cure for his infectious blunder by using the other survivors as test subjects. Meanwhile, Lexx and the sheriff attempt to locate his missing sister, who's stranded somewhere in the battle zone that once was the emergency room. It's a race against time and the ravenous undead. Can they survive the undead before CDC sanitizes the hospital of all infection?

"Witness Protection"
Also available in audiobook!

After witnessing an execution, a resourceful young woman attempts to disappear while being pursued by a hitman and a handsome federal agent.

A helicopter pilot, Jackie Remus, reluctantly agrees to go on a date with one of her clients, but her date is unexpectedly cut short when she witnesses a man being murdered. After narrowly escaping with her life, she is placed into protective custody. When the safe house is breached, Jackie makes a daring escape from both the hired killers and the handsome FBI agent, who wants to return her to protective custody. With a little help from her sly and crafty friend, Monroe, Jackie is convinced she can disappear until the trial. While on her journey to meet with her friend, she solicits help from a few shady but lovable characters along the way. Although she manages to stay one-step ahead of the hired killers, the federal agent remains in hot pursuit. Will Jackie reach Monroe before she's captured by the FBI and returned to protective custody? Or will the hired killers silence her first?

"Town Darling"

After surviving a brutal attack that claims the lives of those she loves, a young woman seeks revenge on a corrupt town.

Going back home is never easy, but for Casey, it means returning to her corrupt hometown where she barely survived a brutal attack. Accompanied by two family friends, she seeks justice for the night that destroyed her life. Her physical scars are nothing compared to her emotional ones, forcing the local sheriff to believe that the town darling is back for revenge. As the conspiracy for her revenge appears to be leading up to the coveted town fair, the sheriff is determined to stop her from fulfilling her vengeful scheme...but guilt over his role on that fateful night continues to haunt him. Will his desperate need for Casey's forgiveness be his undoing? Or will Casey's desire for revenge destroy them both?

"Unconditional"

A young woman puts her life on hold to care for an unstable, highly skilled combat soldier, who believes someone is trying to kill him.

A botched military coup leaves a team of elite fighters injured with one clinging to life in a coma. When Harlan wakes from his coma, he's left with no memory of his past life. His commander's daughter, Indy, takes it upon herself to care for the fallen war hero. She's challenged with more than just his physical care as she combats with not only his memory loss but also his newly found desire for her. His infatuation with her becomes the least of her worries when he sinks back into his role of a combat soldier. Believing his life is in danger, his fighting skills surface, turning him into an unpredictable and dangerous man. Will his memory return to him before Indy is forced to commit him? Or will he finally find his nemesis, "the coyote", and possibly claim the life of an innocent person?

"Witness Protection 2"
The Return of Whiskey Tango Foxtrot

Believing she holds the clue to millions in missing laundered money, a young woman is placed into the protective care of a former Navy SEAL team.

Feeling sorry for her recently separated co-worker, Leeann invites Wiley to join her and her friends on their night out. Little does she know that finding her co-worker murdered is just the beginning of her nightmare. Leeann unknowingly holds the key to fifty million dollars in potentially laundered mob money. With hired killers pursuing her, the FBI places her into a different kind of protective custody. Former Navy SEAL team Whiskey Tango Foxtrot reunites to keep Leeann alive at their secret hideaway. What should be an easy assignment takes an unscheduled turn when secrets, lies, and betrayal threaten to derail their mission. Is the team prepared for a war on their own doorstep? Will Leeann's misguided trust endanger the lives of those sent to protect her?

"Deadly Institution 2"

When blackmail turns into murder, a young woman finds herself caught in the killer's crosshairs.

The small town of Stony Ridge is no stranger to scandal and persecution of the innocent. When a brutal killing shakes the town's prestigious country club, Jacey McMurray seeks help from a self-proclaimed vigilante, Konrad Asher. As her professional and personal worlds collide, Jacey fears the stress of the country club killings have finally taken their toll on Asher. Can a stressed out vigilante stop the killer before he strikes again?

"Witness Protection 3"
Alpha Mike Foxtrot

A helicopter pilot risks her life to help a team of retired Navy SEALs rescue two girls from a killer.

When former Navy SEAL team Whiskey Tango Foxtrot asks for a simple favor, Jackie reluctantly offers her air-taxi services. What could go wrong? What begins as a search and rescue for two girls turns into a fight for survival against a heavily armed drug cartel. Wanted by the law with the cartel in hot pursuit and their home base breached, the team is forced to call in a favor from a questionable ally. Unfortunately, their new safe house isn't what it seems. Without knowing who the real enemy is, can Jackie and the team save their young witnesses from the hands of a killer?

"Awaken the Dead"

A grieving innkeeper struggles to keep her haunted hotel out of foreclosure.

After losing her parents in a suspicious boating accident, Harley Brandon is determined to keep the family hotel out of foreclosure. Unfortunately, the hotel ghosts have other plans. Built with tainted money, the century old Horizon Hotel thrives on a tradition of murder, scandal, and suicide. As the paranormal activity increases to alarming levels, Harley discovers the truth about the hotel and its residents. Can Harley save her friends from the hotel's frightening hidden secrets?

Coming Soon!
"Witness Protection 4"
O-Dark-Hundred

ABOUT THE AUTHOR

Holly Copella has been writing since the age of twelve when her frustration at a book's poor plot drove her to author her own story. Over the last decade, she's written a number of screenplays, some of which she's now adapting into novels. Her fascination with zombies and other darker material lends an edge to her writing, which tends to lean toward horror. As a fan of Agatha Christie, she appreciates the craft of a good plot and the importance of creating significant characters.

Hailing from Pennsylvania, Copella lives in the Endless Mountains on a farm with her rescue horses and other animals. In addition to writing and reading fiction, she enjoys riding horses and traveling to Las Vegas and Disney World.

www.ingramcontent.com/pod-product-compliance
Lightning Source LLC
Chambersburg PA
CBHW072059170626
46813CB00004B/1413